HIS FOUR P
BED

A BEDROOM SECRETS SERIES

EMMA THORNE

Copyright © October, 2015 by Emma Thorne

His Four Poster Bed

Cover by: Najla Qamber Designs
Formatting by: Wyrding Ways Press
Editing by: Wyrding Ways Press

All Rights Reserved. No part of this publication may be reproduced, stored in a retrieval system, or transmitted, in any form or in any means—by electronic, mechanical, photocopying, recording or otherwise—without prior written permission.

This is a work of fiction. Names, characters, places and events are either are the product of the authors' imagination or are used factiously. Any resemblance to actual places, events, and people, living or dead, is purely coincidental.

CHAPTER 1

It was New Year's Eve and I wished I could trade in my party dress for a pair of comfy pajamas and a big glass of wine. Instead, I was dressed to the nines wearing a floor length black gown and silver slippers that would have made any other girl feel like Cinderella.

"Act like you're having fun Odessa and you might enjoy one of these eligible bachelors," my best friend, Shea leaned in and whispered in my ear as we weaved through a sea of tuxedos and ball gowns at the Silver City Fundraiser. The event raised a ridiculous amount of money for Children's Hospital in Seattle where I worked. Unfortunately, so did my ex-boyfriend, Dr. Mike. He was another reason I wanted to stay home.

Shea glittered. Her strawberry blonde hair piled on top of her head, she wore an adorable silver sequined dress and hot red pumps. With lips painted to match her shoes, she looked gorgeous.

Heads turned as we walked through the crowd.

In the center of the ballroom a five-piece band rocked the room from a raised stage. Skinny young men in black tuxedos with their hair slicked back, lots of brass, people dancing and swaying in rhythm with the music as the lead singer crooned out an old Sinatra tune.

It was all very classy, very dignified until a fight broke out on stage.

I saw the first punch.

An extremely hot guy in a tuxedo shouted and popped a short bald man right in the jaw knocking him onto the floor.

Part of the crowd gasped but it happened so quickly I doubted many people had noticed. Then the hot guy stepped right into the spotlight massaging his hand and swinging a bit to the music as a wicked grin crossed his gorgeous face.

I could not tear my eyes away. Tall and wild eyed with closely cropped black hair, the man looked skyward and I noticed the line of a tattoo reaching above the crisp white collar of his shirt. In a flash I found myself wondering what it would be like to run my fingers down the swirl of that tattoo . . .

The singer stuttered on-stage as if he had momentarily forgotten the words to the song, but then the music kicked in again and everything returned to normal, well almost normal.

A swarm of suits surrounded the tuxedo clad

perpetrator. He raised his hands in surrender turning in a slow circle still swinging in time with the music. I noticed nobody touched him as he backed off the stage and disappeared into the crowd.

It was the most interesting thing that happened at this totally appropriate and boring fundraiser and it was over in a minute.

"Did you see that?" I nudged Shea searching for the handsome instigator. He had disappeared into a sea of black and white. In spite of my better judgment, I was extremely disappointed.

"See what?"

"Never mind," I said,

Shea slipped a sky blue cocktail into my hand. "So Sven, that cutie bartender, calls it a sapphire blue," she said, eyebrows dancing. The guy behind the bar looked a bit like a Norse God, flowing long blonde hair and broad shouldered.

We clinked glasses and I took a sip of the sweet blue drink. "Let's toast the perfect midnight kiss," Shea said smiling.

"Let's not," I smiled. "These lips aren't touching anyone tonight, but I'll toast to you." I needed to remind myself that I'd just gotten out of a relationship, searching for or kissing gorgeous troublemakers was not a part of my New Year's plan.

Soon Shea and Sven were engrossed in conversation. From the way he smiled at her, I figured she had found her dance partner for the night. This was my cue to disappear.

"I'm going to go check out the silent auction," I said, deciding that three was a crowd.

"No, stay," she turned and whispered. "Sven wants to introduce you to his friend Tordall. He is off in about fifteen minutes."

I laughed. "Tell Sven and Tordall to have a happy New Year. I'll be fine. I'll meet you in the lobby at midnight."

"You sure?" She looked a little pained but her eyes darted back to her blonde Viking.

"Don't do anything I wouldn't do," I said, giving her a quick kiss on the cheek.

"I intend to do many things you wouldn't do," she laughed. "Please try to have fun."

I made my way across the dance floor. According to the oversized clock above the band, I officially had one hour to kill before I could turn into a pumpkin.

The silent auction was mercifully quiet. The bidding closed soon and most people were in line at the buffet or dancing by now. I browsed past mini posters describing ski vacations, winery tours, and cruise ships to Alaska, the Caribbean, and Mexico. Finally, I reached the last table filled with artwork ranging from quilting projects to oil paintings.

One display caught my eye. Under a single spotlight on a velvet black pillar stood a collection of three golden bird cages each containing a unique sculpture of a bird. There was a silver canary with painted yellow wings and glittering eyes. A bejeweled parrot that looked as if it was about to take flight and a shimmering silver white dove.

"Beauty Caged" by Theo Manhattan (Donated by M. Amador)

The starting bid was $5,000.

Pricey, I thought, recognizing the donor name. The Amador family sponsored the Silver City event and a lot of other philanthropic events in the city. I was pretty sure they owned this hotel and half the waterfront downtown.

"Aren't they gorgeous?" a voice beside me interrupted my thoughts. "Though it seems wrong to cage such beauty."

A tall good looking man stood beside me wearing a custom made tuxedo that hugged his body in all the right places. He raised his eyebrows and smiled at me, eyes crinkling in the corners. My legs went weak. I took a breath realizing I was staring into the deep brown eyes of the man who had thrown the first punch.

"Do you like art?" he asked, taking a sip of his cocktail.

"Uh yes," I said, struggling for words. "Do you like fighting in public?"

He pursed his lips and nodded to me. "You saw my little show."

"Is that what you call it?" I asked managing to turn away from his gaze. This man's body screamed sex, I felt my cheeks flush wondering what it would be like to lock lips with him at midnight.

"I call it a disagreement," he shrugged.

"You punched a man."

"No, first I told him to mind his own fucking business and then I punched him," he winked. "I'm Marco." He held out his hand and I stared at it, uncertain if I wanted to make contact. He dropped his hand when I didn't shake it. "I have a confession," he said. Unfazed he picked up the bid sheet and scrawled something on the paper. "I've been watching you tonight."

"You've been watching me," I repeated, his words flattering and alarming me all at the same time. "That's a bit creepy."

"Too creepy?" he said, smiling an adorable, sexy smile. "Or just a tiny bit flattering?"

"Maybe a smidge," I said, a smile escaping me. Damn. It was hard to stay cold next to the heat of his body.

"May I offer you another cocktail?"

"Do I look like a woman you can ply with a simple cocktail?"

"Absolutely not," he said, his brown eyes glittering with mischief. "You look infinitely more difficult."

A white-coated waiter walked by and the man tapped him on the shoulder. "Thank you John, I'll take this," the man said. He took the waiter's whole tray.

The waiter looked a bit flustered, eyes darting from the man to me. "Yes, sir, thank you sir, of course," he said, disappearing into the sea of people.

"Who are you?" I asked, watching the waiter walk away.

"Marco," he said, shrugging and handing me a cocktail before setting the tray beside the birdcages.

"Marco who?" I asked, wheels turning in my mind. He looked familiar but I assumed that was because he'd been on stage. Even so, I felt as though I knew him somehow.

"My name is Marco Amador," he said the last name slowly. "I thought you knew."

My stomach dropped. I knew the Amador family was the host of the night's event, but I'd never met the hot-headed heir to the family fortune. I'd heard some whispers about the family since they were one of the hospital's biggest donors. The fact Marco looked like a movie star was something the rumor mill had failed to share. I had always imagined a sullen, skinny young man hiding from the press, and here was this beautiful specimen that made me want to chuck my New Year's resolution and do more than kiss at midnight.

"You are Marco Amador," I repeated, gesturing to the room. "Why are you punching people at your own party?"

"It's my father's party," he said, looking sheepish. The expression did not suit him entirely. "And the guy had it coming, he's an asshole and needed to understand that I don't take orders from anyone."

"I see," I said.

"That sounded rather dramatic didn't it," he said.

This man had a strength that made it hard for me to focus. In spite of my better efforts, I found my eyes continually drifting to the cut of his jacket, the way his biceps strained his suit in just the right places. I was suddenly grateful that Shea had talked me into wearing my favorite black dress. It was floor length with a plunging neckline that revealed my cleavage. I wore one of my mother's necklaces, a long pendant my father had given her long ago before their split. The chain glittered between my breasts and I noticed how Marco's eyes drifted to my skin.

"The truth is, I hate parties," he said.

"You don't like the crowds?"

"I don't like meaningless conversation."

"Well, this is a rather meaningless conversation."

"It doesn't have to be," he said, his brown eyes locking on mine.

My heart pounded. I felt as though we were dancing some verbal tango. Each phrase pulling me one step closer to this gorgeous man. I tried to remind myself that I was not here to meet anyone, to make out with anyone, to fall into bed with anyone.

"Would you like to go on a walk with me?" Marco asked.

"Through the crowd you dislike so much," I said.

"I know someplace quiet and I have a question for you."

"A meaningless question?"

"Hardly. It's quite important. I must know the name of the most beautiful woman in this room."

"Wow, that's quite a line."

"It's not a line."

He stared at me, his gaze unwavering. My mouth went dry while the rest of me dripped wet.

"You are showing a lot of your cards tonight, Mr. Amador," I said, feeling breathless at the ache of desire between my legs.

"I'd like to show you more." He stepped closer.

"Is that so."

"I promise this bad boy will behave like a perfect gentleman, I won't even glance at your bare ankle as you walk in that ridiculously beautiful dress that looks like it could come undone at a glance."

I wanted Marco to reach out and un-tie the halter knot at the base of my neck. I wanted my dress to fall to my feet and stand naked before this gorgeous man in nothing but my high heels.

"My name is Odessa," I said, holding out my hand. "Odessa Starr. Dr. Starr actually, I work at Children's. I'm in research."

"Odessa Starr." He made my name sound like a dirty word and I liked it. "A beautiful name for a beautiful woman." He held out his arm. "Shall we walk Dr. Starr?"

I looked at Marco Amador as if we were the only two people in the room. He had given me a choice that night but I felt like my body had chosen for me the moment Marco stood beside me in the dark.

"Yes, let's take a walk," I said, taking his arm.

Marco led me across the dance floor and I knew in that moment that I would follow this man anywhere. I just had no idea how far away he would lead me.

CHAPTER 2

The crowd parted for us as if we were royalty.

I glanced back at the bar and caught a glimpse of Shea, her eyes were wide as she watched us leave. Sven her Nordic bartender was chatting away beside her. My ex, Dr. Mike, stood in the middle of the dance floor, his jaw tightening as we briefly made eye contact. It wasn't hard to read his expression. He was none too pleased to see me on the arm of a stranger, there would be hell to pay in awkwardness after this New Year's party.

Marco led me out of the ballroom into the white marbled lobby of the Four Seasons Hotel.

The hotel had been remodeled a few years ago, the old building demolished and replaced by a sleek skyscraper. The original marble still graced the main floor giving it an old world elegance that contrasted with the modern lines of the building. A heavy chandelier hung in the middle of the lobby.

Marco walked behind the front desk to elevators that would have looked like a service entrance if it weren't for the discrete sign that read "Private Residence."

I stopped in my tracks. "Where are we going?"

He squinted his eyes and leaned in whispering in my ear. "Don't tell anyone but I live upstairs."

"You have a private elevator." I was definitely out of my league here.

"It's better that way. I like to fly under the radar."

"I see." My heart hammering, I thought about what it might be like to walk arm and arm with this man through his private residence, through the front door, past the living room, and straight into his bedroom. "An elevator ride is not much of a walk," I said.

"I thought you might like to see the view from upstairs."

Upstairs. Did I want to go upstairs with this man? Yes. Yes, I did.

"The view. You know in college, guys used to offer to show me their fish tank."

He grinned. "Did that work? I could get a tank."

I laughed. "No, it didn't work, and it won't work tonight." I looked up into those brown eyes knowing it was going to take a lot of will power to resist touching this beautiful man. I was used to feeling in control of my urges and desires. The attraction I felt to Marco felt raw and uncontainable. With every breath, I could smell his scent, a musky cologne that made me think of sex on silky sheets. I was used to picking safe and predictable men and here I was standing in front of the dangerous and unknown.

Finger poised over the up button, Marco looked at me. “Dr. Starr it’s your call? Would you like to go upstairs with me, or should we return to the party?”

I exhaled and took a deep breath thinking of another hour in the dull ballroom dodging Dr. Mike. I decided that I could handle myself and this man. “The view. I’d like to see the view.”

“Excellent.” Marco pressed the up button.

The doors opened and we stepped inside. There were only two buttons to choose from. Lobby and a single button with the letter P on it.

“P for Penthouse? I asked, pointing to the destination.

“Some call it that,” Marco said. He looked a bit embarrassed.

We stood side by side in silence as the elevator whirred skyward. It seemed to go both incredibly fast and impossibly high. My ears popped as the doors opened revealing a large slate and wood entryway that framed a bank of windows facing the night sky. It looked as though you could reach out and run your fingers through the stars.

“That’s quite a view,” I said walking towards the glass. I slowed as I reached the edge, looking down made me a bit dizzy. Below us I could see the lights of the city, the black waters of Puget Sound and the shadow of the Olympic Peninsula.

"Is it better than a fish tank?" Marco called from behind me. I heard glasses clinking and assumed he was making us another cocktail.

"It's the edge of the world," I said, looking back and forth. "No neighbors up this high."

Marco approached with crystal glasses filled with the now familiar Sapphire Blue cocktail. "I muddled the oranges myself," he said, handing me one.

"Look at you, the bartender."

"I got skills," he said, raising an eyebrow before turning to look out the window. I tried not to stare at his profile, he was gorgeous in a classic way, but the hint of that tattoo was driving me mad. I knew his comment about skills was a reference to his drink making, but I couldn't help but wonder what kind of skills he might have between the sheets, with that mouth and those hands . . . I took a big sip of my drink hoping the cool liquid might temper the fire currently smoldering in my core.

Marco broke the silence, exhaling softly. "The quiet up here. It's the thing I love best about this place. Up here it feels as though I can truly be alone."

He spoke with an intensity that made me want to ask

more about his desire for a solitary life. There was a sadness in his voice.

"You could walk around here naked and no one would see," I said, unable to keep from flirting.

"Would you like to test that theory out?"

"No thank you," I said, softly but smiling what I knew was a wicked grin. This man made me want to do delicious things. What had I gotten myself into and how was I going to get out of here without taking off any of my clothes?

"Tell me about your research at the hospital," Marco said, as we stood in front of the windows.

"Research, yes." I took a drink. "I'm lead researcher on the Smart Chemo trials at Children's. We do genetic analysis of patients and treat the child holistically instead of subjecting them to protocols based on their cancer. So, instead of following some check list for bone cancer, or brain cancer we engineer a solution that we hope will support the genetic makeup of that child."

He smiled as I talked. "And it's working?"

"Oh God yes, I mean I can't say it's working, but the data is incredibly compelling and I am very hopeful about the next round of patients . . ." My voice trailed off and I glanced at my drink a bit self-conscious. "I can go on and on about this."

"You are passionate," he said, looking at me. "It's wonderful to see."

"I love my work. When I went to medical school I assumed I'd end up with a private practice, but I've found working behind the scenes engineering this type of change is," I struggled for the word.

"Inspiring?" He said.

"Yes, it inspires me," I said. "I can't imagine doing anything else."

"Would you like to sit?" He pointed to a comfortable white couch in front of the fireplace.

I took a seat while Marco took off his jacket and untied his bow tie. "Are you done with the party?" I asked.

"I don't want to go back downstairs," he said, sighing. "You can of course, but I think I'll stay here and ring in the New Year." He grabbed a small controller and hit a button, igniting the fireplace. As he reached I caught another glimpse of the green blue tattoo at his throat.

"That's some ink," I said, eyebrows raised.

"My father hates it." Marco grinned and pulled the collar back on his shirt. I could see that the green loop was the top edge of a swirling power circle that extended down his body. My mouth went dry. Ink. Why did the man have to be inked? I loved it.

"Does it mean something?" I asked resisting the urge to touch his skin.

"I started the tattoo after my mother died in high school and I've been adding to it ever since."

"I'm sorry about your mother," I said.

"So am I." He smiled and even though it had clearly been years since he had lost her I could see the pain he still lived with.

"So, it covers your shoulder then? The tattoo?" I tried to act nonchalant but I was dying to touch this man.

"It's a sleeve," he said pointing to his right arm.

"Nice," I said breathless. I could feel myself getting wet. I was such a sucker for a tattooed arm. There was something incredibly sexy about a man who had committed to express himself like that.

Next to the fireplace were some built in bookshelves. A painting of the ocean hung above the fireplace.

"You like art?" I said, nodding at the painting.

Marco took a sip of his drink and smiled at me before answering. "I collect beautiful things."

"And I can't imagine you'd ever consider a woman a thing."

"Women are much too powerful to collect," he said. "Do you know why I purchased those cages downstairs for the auction?"

"You like birds?"

Marco grinned, his eyes crinkling in such an adorable way I wanted to lean forward and kiss him, but I didn't. "I do like birds, but no. I purchased the collection to remind me of something."

"Is that so?" I felt as though the distance between us was shrinking with every word.

"I don't believe in cages," he said. "I don't think people should be trapped by their identity, their life or the people they love."

Marco leaned towards me and I could feel my body tense up as he moved closer.

"You don't believe in physical cages, or is this some sort of metaphor?" I said, my heart hammering in my chest.

"I don't believe in controlling anyone who doesn't want to be controlled," he said, standing in front of me offering me his hand. I took it and stood before him. He traced a fingertip across my cheek and I inhaled closing my eyes in spite of myself. He had so much confidence, so much strength in his touch.

When my body stopped tingling, I looked into his eyes wondering if he knew that being this close to him sent my mind spinning with all his talk of control.

I wanted him but I couldn't, I wouldn't I shouldn't. To distract myself, I looked over Marco's shoulder through an open door at the end of the hall. I could see the edge of what looked like an ornate bed, a single wooden post in my view.

"That's my bedroom," he said, his voice low, his hand softly stroking my cheek.

"You have a beautiful bed," I said, knowing I was treading on dangerous ground.

"I told you, I love beautiful things," he paused for a moment his gaze never leaving my face. "Would you like to see the view from my bedroom Odessa Starr?"

I nodded. Forming words had suddenly become very difficult.

Marco stood and took my hand walking backwards and leading me across the room. "I promised I would be a gentleman," he said. "I always keep my promises."

"I am holding you to it."

"It may get more difficult the closer I get you to that bed."

"I suppose we will both need to be strong then," I said, my eyes never leaving his.

He opened his bedroom door and dropped my hand stepping away from me.

The bedroom faced the black water and the stars. There was no one in the world high enough to see into this room. No one who could see what happened in this room inside this four poster bed.

A deep dark wood, the four posters were tall and carved in a swirling pattern that reached towards the ceiling connected at the top with horizontal pieces of wood. I imagined this bed could have resided in a palace with silk curtains enclosing clandestine lovers.

Marco's bed had no curtains. The bed was bare and exposed staring out into the star filled night. I wondered what it would be like to lay with Marco between the sheets and stare into the sky. This was a bed to make love in and fuck. My cheeks burned as I fantasized about Marco above me, silk scarves in his hand ready to tie me down, to own me, to—

"Do you like the bed?" He asked, smiling.

"It's quite a bed," I said, hoping my voice sounded steady.

"You know we are here for the view," he said, stepping towards me.

"You didn't mean to show me your bedroom?"

"You're the one who wanted to see it."

He stood in front of me only inches away, and I no

longer wanted to fight the attraction. "Would you just shut up and kiss me."

We crashed into each other with an intensity and a need that I had never felt before. His lips were strong and firm; I felt him harden as he pressed his body against mine, his arms around my waist and on the back of my head.

"It's not midnight," he whispered, taking a breath.

"I don't care."

He nodded and I moaned softly as he kissed me again. At the touch of his skin against mine I felt a bolt of electricity move through my body straight to my core. My legs weak and my pussy wet, I knew right then that my future with this man would contain more than a single kiss. I turned and looked at the four poster bed. It called to us like a siren.

And then there was the sound of heels on the stone floor and a woman's voice.

"Excuse me Marco, or is this a bad time?"

Breathless and reeling with desire, I pulled away from Marco to find myself staring at a tall, thin African American woman. She was willowy and beautiful wearing a long red dress and a set of black pearls around her neck. She stared at us, her expression unreadable, bored almost. I was so embarrassed.

Marco glanced between the two of us. “Of course it’s a bad time,” he said, his voice tense.

“I can go,” I said, moving.

“No, don’t.” Marco grabbed my hand, but I shook him off.

“I apologize,” the woman said, her voice accented and lilting, South African. “I did not expect you to take a guest home tonight. Do you think that wise?”

“I’m leaving,” I said, slapping Marco’s hand away when he reached for me a second time. Suddenly I felt foolish for thinking a man like Marco would be uncomplicated and not a liar. It was clear that Marco and this woman shared a history. She knew him well and I was just some idiot he’d picked up at the party downstairs. I had no problem taking a lover when I wanted but I demanded total honesty. I would not be betrayed by some hot billionaire even if he was sex in a tuxedo. I didn’t care how good he kissed or how big his cock was, and from the bulge I had felt in his pants, it was pretty damn big.

“Good night Marco,” I said, making it to the elevator and hitting the down button before he could reach me. The doors opened.

“Christ Veronica,” I heard Marco mutter then shouting. “Odessa, please wait,” he called to me. The clock above his mantle began to chime.

"Happy New Year," I said, as the countdown to midnight began. Like Cinderella I wanted to escape the ball.

As the doors closed I believed my short lived relationship with the lying, cheating Marco Amador had come to an end; little did I know that things had barely just begun.

CHAPTER 3

The first gift arrived the next morning.

I awoke to a gentle rapping on my door. It was 9:00 a.m., I usually rose early and went for a morning run before my shift at the hospital, but I suppose the Sapphire Blue's and late nights at the hospital had finally caught up with me.

I thought of Marco as I walked to my door, the memory of his kiss stirring up a range of emotions from desire to anger. He had gotten me so turned on and pissed off in such a short amount of time. I was glad I had a day of work to distract myself.

Someone rapped again.

"Coming?" I said, pulling on a short robe.

Billie, the building manager and my friend, stood outside my door holding a large black box in her arms, two other boxes sat at her feet. Her dark hair back in a ponytail, she wore a flannel shirt and orange vest. She looked as though she were about to head out for a day of camping or hiking, which was quite likely. I liked the idea of camping but knew myself well enough to know that high heeled boots were frowned upon in the great outdoors. It was not my scene.

"Happy New Year sunshine," Billie said, grinning. "Special delivery." Billie handed me a large black box topped with a thick white bow.

"This isn't from UPS," I said, feeling confused and sleepy. Billie had so much energy I often felt terribly lazy in her presence. She'd probably already painted one of the units and baked some homemade granola for an endurance hike with her gorgeous boyfriend, Vincent.

"Nope," she said, smiling. "It is not UPS." Billie walked past me stacking two of the packages under my window.

"Where exactly did these come from?" I asked as she walked past me to retrieve the last box.

"You tell me," Billie said, wiping her hands off as if they were dusty when everything was inside my apartment. "You have an admirer from last night's party?"

My head throbbed for a moment as the memory of Marco bubbled again to the surface. It had to be him, there was no other logical explanation, but how had he found me? Didn't billionaires have a way of finding what they wanted? After all he said he collected beautiful things.

My cheeks flushed and I felt a wave of rage roll through my body. How dare he track me down. I was not something to be collected.

"Who delivered these to the building if it wasn't UPS?" I asked.

"Well, a woman came by this morning in a limo." Billie slowed her pronunciation of limo, eyebrows raised.

My body tensed. "Wait . . . A woman?"

"Yes, really pretty. Tall, African American. She looked like a model. Are you going to open them or what?"

The memory of being awkwardly interrupted was just as strong as the memory of Marco's kiss. What a bastard.

"I don't know what I'm going to do with them," I said, wrapping my robe tighter around my waist. The woman in the limo had to be Veronica, which made no sense. She had not seemed pleased at all to find us lip locked in his bedroom. I had assumed she was his lover, or his sometimes lover. Either way this was bizarre. Why was she delivering gifts to my apartment?

"Did she say anything when she dropped off the boxes?" I asked.

"She knew you lived in The Holiday but not the unit," Billie said. "She knew your name and that you were a doctor. She described you to a tee. Down to your plunging black dress." Billie grinned. "Who is she?"

"A very rich man's girlfriend I think," I said. I picked

up one of the boxes untying the white bow. It was deceptively heavy. The box was made of thick cardboard. I've always had a thing for beautiful packages. Card stock, stationary, letters, it's one of my indulgences.

I glanced over my shoulder at Billie as she stood watching me like a curious spectator.

"Oh, sorry," Billie said. "You want privacy?"

"I don't know what I want," I blurted. I had to open that damn box. I took off the black lid. The box was filled with heavy tissue paper. I saw the glint of gold beneath the paper and pulled one of the bird cages from the auction. I was staring into the glittering black eyes of a yellow canary.

"A bird?" Billie said, wrinkling her nose. "I mean it's pretty, but did you order a bunch of birds online?"

"No, I didn't," I said, moving to the next package unwrapping the parrot followed by the dove.

Marco had sent me all three birds. He had clearly bought his donation at the silent auction and sent the art to me. I placed all three of the cages on the wide window seat of my apartment that faces the alley.

There was a single card inside the last package embossed with an A.

"Amador," I muttered under my breath.

Then this:

Allow me the opportunity to explain myself.

I would never betray or cage a woman as fierce and beautiful as you.

Marco

He'd written his phone number in parenthesis at the bottom of the card.

"Did some man send you birds?" Billie asked, arms crossed, eyes narrowing as she took in the sculptures in the room. "I mean it's cool, but different."

"Seems like it," I said, not sure I wanted to reveal anything more about the mysterious delivery which I was most certainly returning as soon as I got home from work.

"Well, this is interesting." I heard Shea's voice and turned to see her standing behind Billie. Wearing work out gear, her long strawberry blonde hair in a high ponytail, she looked ready to meet one of her fitness clients. She had probably popped in on her way out the door. Shea tended to tack runs onto the start and end of her work day. She was in such good shape it was ridiculous.

"Is all this artsy shit from Marco Amador?" Eyes bugging she picked up the dove, her nose wrinkling. "What ever happened to flowers?"

"It's not artsy shit," I said, feeling like I had lost control of my personal life in a mere twenty-four hours. So much for New Year's resolutions to keep things simple. "It's art."

"So, what are you going to do with your *art* then?" Shea asked.

"Return it," I said, turning to face my friends. "But first, I'm going to go to work. Thanks for bringing this stuff upstairs Billie."

"Hey, anytime," Billie said. "I'll see you girls later." She walked into the hall closing the door behind her.

"I mean who sends boxes of birds after meeting a woman once?" Shea asked.

"A billionaire who is used to getting what he wants," I said, going to my closet.

"Oh, I get it." Shea followed me. "I see what's going on. Marco Amador wants you and you don't want to want him back." She paused then tilted her head. "But you do want him, that's why you're being so pissed off and weird about this. What really happened last night?"

I'd given Shea some details but not all of them. I was pretty embarrassed about the whole situation to tell the truth.

"I don't want him," I said pulling my dark hair back

with a headband and slipping on a pencil skirt and blouse. I made it a point to dress up for work unless I was assisting in a surgery.

"You are rattled by him," Shea said, grinning. "Odessa Starr, used to being in the driver's seat, met someone who she might not be able to control."

"Please," I said, trying to ignore the pit in my stomach. Was Shea right? Was that why my heart was pounding at the memory of Marco? Was I afraid to be out of control? If I was honest with myself, I was conflicted about those damn birds. Half of me wanted to send the birds back, another part of me wanted to dial the number scrawled beneath his name and tell him to send the car and driver back right away. I wanted to hear his explanation. I wanted a date with this man in his four poster bed.

"I'm not afraid of him," I said. "I thought we had chemistry but I think he's a player and you know that doesn't work for me."

"Takes a player to know a player," Shea said, rocking back on her heels.

I shot her a look, annoyed.

"I'm just saying, you aren't exactly one to settle down. In fact you have broken hearts on a regular basis ever since I met you."

"I don't break hearts. I am very clear about what I am looking for."

"And when it gets messy you leave."

"I have to work," I said, reaching for my purse and holding open the door.

"You always do," Shea said, giving me a quick kiss on the cheek. "You know I love you. I just think it might not be the end of the world if you found a guy that actually rattles you a bit."

"I'm not looking to be rattled."

"Um, I think you are," Shea laughed and give me a quick kiss on the cheek. "See you later chica. I gotta run." As I watched Shea run down the hall I thought about what she'd said. I did enjoy men, I enjoyed having lovers and when the relationship had run its course I ended things.

I'd seen what happened when a woman gave up her identity for a man. I'd watched my mother collapse under the weight of my father's affairs and their messy divorce. He'd been gone for over ten years and she still insisted he would come back to her bed someday. I never wanted to depend on someone like that.

As I walked down the hall to the back alley, where I parked my car, I reflected on how lucky I was. I had friends, a great apartment at The Holiday, and work that made me want to get out of bed in the morning.

And when it was time to take another lover, I would. It just wouldn't be Marco Amador. I was returning those damn birds tonight.

CHAPTER 4

As soon as I walked through the glass doors of the hospital, I felt better about the situation with Marco. Work was the great equalizer in my life, it gave me focus and purpose. I had patients who needed me and didn't care what bad decisions I'd made the night before. My research landed outside the boundary of my personal life. I'd made a huge mistake mixing business with pleasure with Dr. Mike and I was determined to learn from my mistakes.

I walked into the front lobby and nodded to the volunteers at the front desk, my badge displayed. The lobby of Children's was filled with bright sculptures and underwater creates, an enormous orca statue hung overhead. I passed families waiting for urgent care admittance or to pick up prescriptions in the pharmacy.

That's when I saw him; I stopped in my tracks.

Marco Amador stood at the end of the foyer right next to Marcia Kim, the president of the board of directors. Marcia waved me over. There was no way to slip away without appearing rude.

"Good morning Marcia, hello Mr. Amador," I said, doing a very bad job of hiding my surprise. What was he doing here in my workplace? I flipped my smile back on and hoped I looked poised instead of rattled.

It was hard not to notice the way Marco looked. He wore a thin black turtleneck, most likely cashmere and dark blue jeans that hugged his body. I caught a glance of his shoes, they looked expensive.

"Mr. Amador has come to deliver a donation to the hospital and it's earmarked for your chemo study," Marcia said, positively glowing. "It's just wonderful, a wonderful surprise."

I wasn't sure how many zeros were on the check, but I figured it had to be generous to elicit this type of giddiness from Marcia. She was not known for being touchy feely, quite the opposite in fact.

I immediately felt conflicted. Dollar signs meant we could help more children, but this windfall came from the man I'd mistakenly made out with the night before.

"How wonderful," I said. "You'll have to thank your father for me. I'm glad the fundraiser was a success." I said emphasizing the word father and knowing it was a bit of a low blow, but I'd be dammed if I was going to fall to the man's feet and thank him for being born to a rich man. I appreciated the donation, but if he thought this would buy me off somehow, he had another thing coming.

Marco flinched at my words and opened his mouth as if he wanted to say something more but thought better of it.

"Actually, no," Marcia said. "The Amador foundation will send us the check from the gala next week. Mr. Amador has given a personal donation to the foundation this morning. Isn't that wonderful?"

"A personal donation?" I said, eyebrows raised. It was admirable for him to share some of his funds with us, but it didn't change the fact that he was a rich man from a rich family. He was able to donate because of who he was, not because of what he had accomplished in life.

"Yes," Marco said, cheeks burning. "I had thought this would be an anonymous donation."

"That's admirable," I said. The fact he wanted to donate quietly was interesting. It didn't change things, but I had to give him some credit.

"Oh, we won't share beyond this group," Marcia stated.

"I apologize Odessa," Marco said. "I didn't think you would be here this morning."

"I'm sorry, do you two know each other?" Marcia said eyes darting between us.

"No," I said. As Marco said "Yes."

"Yes," I repeated as he changed his answer to "No."

"I see," Marcia said, clearly not seeing anything at all.

Marco and I faced each other saying nothing.

"I'd like to give Mr. Amador a tour but I have a meeting that starts in ten minutes," Marcia said. "Odessa would you mind?"

"That won't be necessary," Marco said.

"No, I insist," Marcia said. "I know it's an anonymous donation but at the very least you could see how your funds will be used. Please, let us show you the facility. It's the least we can do."

"All right then," he said, looking at me his brown eyes a bit wide.

"I'll leave you two to it," Marcia said. "Good day, Mr. Amador, and thank you again for your generosity. We can do some wonderful things with this type of funding. Can't we Dr. Starr?"

"Yes, of course," I said.

Marco and I both watched Marcia leave.

I waited until she was out of ear shot.

"Seriously?" I asked, stepping closer to him keeping my voice low. "An anonymous donation?"

"You have to believe me," he said. "I did not intend you to find out about this."

"Oh please," I whispered, moving closer. "You send

me bird cages, expensive bird cages. An entire collection and you expect me to think that you are trying to be low profile."

"It is a holiday, I assumed you would not be at the office. I was telling you the truth. And as for the gift, I felt I owed you an apology and an explanation."

"Why did Veronica deliver them? What is the deal with you two?"

"So, you do care," he said, a sly smile crossing his face.

"No, I don't care. I don't care one bit," I said, my heart pounding.

"Veronica works with me," he said.

"She works with you or for you?" I said, remembering the way she had stood there in that red clinging dress. "You expect me to believe it's just a work thing. Do all your coworkers dress like that and have access to your bedroom?" The humiliation of kissing Marco in front of Veronica came over me and I felt stupid again for being sucked in by Marco's good looks and money. "You know what? Don't answer that. It's not my business, forget it."

"Odessa, you must forgive me if I missed my mark here."

"You missed more than your mark. I appreciate the donation but it has nothing to do with me. It can't. You understand that."

"I gave you the cages because they are beautiful, like you and the hospital was a spontaneous decision. I woke up this morning inspired by your passion for these children. You were not meant to find out about it but you were my inspiration."

"I inspired you," I repeated trying not to let my gaze drift from his face to those strong arms. Damn, I loved the way the turtleneck hugged his body.

He stepped toward me and lowered his voice as a family sat down in chairs right in front of us. "Should we go somewhere private?"

"I don't think that would be appropriate," I said. "You and I are safer in a crowd."

"Fair enough," He said, flashing me a grin. "You must believe me that I woke up today and I wanted to do something on my own, to act. I've been silent for too long and being with you last night, however brief, has given me something I haven't had in a long time."

"What is that," I said, trying to sound disinterested and failing.

"Hope," he said.

"I gave you hope."

"Yes. Hope that I can make a difference. That I can do

good in this world away from my family's shadow. You do good every day, why shouldn't I try as well," he said, looking pained. "I sound like an idiot."

"No, you sound . . .," I paused and smiled. "Inspired. I think you are full of shit but you do sound inspired."

Marco wrinkled his nose. "So, the birds may have been too much."

"You think?"

"I apologize if they made you uncomfortable. It's been a while since I've met someone like you."

"You know I can't be bought."

"I would never try."

"Good," I said.

And we stood like that face to face. He was so arrogant but clearly felt out of his element. I wanted to know more about Veronica and his desire to break free from his family, but I had a job to do and playing therapist to a hot billionaire with Daddy issues was very low on my list of things to do.

"Would you like a tour," I asked, gesturing towards the doors. "It would have to be quick, I have patients to see."

"Patients in your trial, or children you are evaluating for the next round?"

"The next round," I said, smiling. "You were listening

to me last night."

"Every word," he said, his eyes locking with mine again. And suddenly I felt like we were no longer standing in the crowded lobby of the hospital. The buzz and the noise of families and children surrounding me faded; I felt as though there was a single spotlight on us.

"Marco, I'm sorry, you seem nice . . ." But I can't see you again, the words were right there, just sitting on the tip of my tongue, ready to be rolled out. After all he did seem nice and I didn't understand his strange relationship with Veronica or his family, but he had listened to me. He was an amazing kisser and our brief encounter had resulted in a hefty donation to the hospital. None of this was bad.

"Before you decide anything," he said. "See me tonight. We can talk."

"I'm not sure that's a good idea."

"I'll take a rain check on the tour," he said. "You are busy and I would rather you focus your energy on your young patients than me. Come see me tonight. I'll send a car."

"I'll drive myself thank you," I said, without thinking about the implication of my comment. Marco's face broke out into a wide smile.

"Excellent," he said. "The woman will drive herself

and I will see you this evening."

Over Marco's shoulder I caught a glimpse of Dr. Mike. He stood by the elevators with a pained expression on his face, he clearly had noticed my conversation with the young, hot billionaire. I hoped the acoustics in the lobby were playing in my favor. I did not need Dr. Mike questioning me about Marco after I'd just convinced him I wasn't ready to date anyone.

"Thank you for your donation," I said, unsure what to say next. "Truly, it will allow us to do some wonderful work."

"Of course, yes. It was my pleasure," he said. He looked at me knowingly before extending his hand. Just hearing the word pleasure come from this man's lips made me feel a bit unsteady.

"Thank you for giving me another chance."

"I won't change my mind," I said, knowing I sounded weak.

"Of course not."

I shook his hand and his skin felt warm against mine, his hands were large and strong. He nodded and turned walking straight out of the building and through the glass doors.

So, Marco Amador had been inspired by our brief time

together. Was he being sincere or was this some sort of bizarre method of seduction? He clearly was not used to dating *normal* women; his over the top antics demonstrated that clearly. His decision to shower me with bird cages was more bizarre than sweet. He said he loved being alone, but clearly he craved something more in his life. He was a complicated man and damn if he wasn't hot.

"Paging Dr. Starr," the sound of the overhead speaker snapped me to attention. I had patients I needed to see, data to review. The page seemed like a sign to me, a reminder of the life that I needed to focus on. I immediately felt guilty for standing in the lobby like a star struck school girl. This was why I had made a New Year's resolution to stay single and focus on myself.

Marco may have talked me into seeing him again, but this strange relationship needed to end tonight.

CHAPTER 5

"Odessa Starr, I'm here to see Marco Amador," I said, to one of the bellmen who hovered near Marco's private elevator.

The bellman, a slip of a boy who looked like a college kid earning extra money looked a little nervous. "I'm sorry, I'm not allowed to reveal the names of our guests."

"I was here last night," I said. "I was a guest of Mr. Amador's and I have something to return to him. And he's a resident, not a guest." I nodded to the stack of black packages that I'd carried from the car.

The bellman seemed to consider me and I wondered if he was trying to figure out if I was Marco's type. Marco claimed Veronica was a co-worker, but I truly had no idea about the number of women who traveled up and down his private elevator, no pun intended.

"Excuse me for a moment," the boy said, giving me the once over. I resisted the urge to tell him to take a picture since it lasted longer. He was only doing his job. I supposed every billionaire needed a gatekeeper.

I checked my makeup in the mirror behind the front desk while I waited. I'd touched up my cat's eyeliner and red lipstick in the break room before leaving work. My white blouse still looked crisp, even after rounds; my pencil skirt had survived the day as well. My hair pulled back into a sleek ponytail revealing gold hoop earrings completed my look; I wanted to look good, but professional. I also wasn't going to change after our morning run-in. I did not want Marco to misunderstand my intent. This was business.

The boy returned holding a small notebook. "May I see your ID?" He asked as he paged through the book.

"Are you serious," I deadpanned, pulling my license out of my wallet. "What are you TSA?"

His finger poised on the page he glance up at me, eyes wide. "I'm so sorry Ms. Starr, your name is on the list," his cheeks flushed. "I'm sorry, I'm new. I just need to validate you are who you say you are this one time. My apologies."

"Not your fault, and glad I'm on the list . . ." I eyeballed the boy's name tag. "Todd. Thank you, I realize you are just following orders."

"I'm so sorry Ms. Starr. You are definitely allowed upstairs; I apologize for detaining you."

"What exactly does his little black book say about me?" I said, eyebrows raised.

Todd tightened his smile. "I'm messing this all up, please don't tell Mr. Amador I detained you. I'll carry your luggage upstairs."

"Thank you Todd," I said, as he lifted the boxes and escorted me to the private elevator. "And it's not my luggage."

"Of course, Ma'am," Todd said.

"I'm returning a gift,' I said, nodding at the boxes. "Not staying. Nope. Not staying. And please don't call me Ma'am."

"Yes, Ma'am. I mean Miss," Todd said. Eyes fixed on the doors as we whirred skyward, I realized I was trying to explain myself to a college boy. He clearly counted me as one of Marco's conquests, whatever Marco had put in his book had marked me as a woman with a pass upstairs. The thought filled me with an odd sense of pride in spite of myself.

Oh well, Todd the bellman could think what he wanted.

The elevator chimed.

"Here you are, Ma'am," Todd said, arm extended he held open the doors. "I'll bring your bags."

"Not my . . . never mind," I said, smiling.

I turned to face the entryway. It looked even more beautiful than I remembered, without the haze of Sapphire Blue clouding my mind. The walls were exposed brick with high ceilings and wide wood beams. The contrast between the raw materials on the walls and the luxurious marble floor was stunning. This place was so much different than the rundown charm of my apartment at The Holiday. I needed to say my piece, whatever that was, and get in and out.

I took a breath knowing that beautiful things have a way of changing people's minds.

I heard the elevator doors chime and turned to catch a glimpse of Bellboy Todd waving as the doors closed. I was alone in the lobby with Marco's gifts beside me.

"I am so glad to see you. You have no idea," Marco said, stepping into my view from the kitchen.

Damn.

I took a breath.

Beware beautiful things and beautiful men, I thought. Marco stood in front of me wearing the same thin black turtleneck and dark blue jeans from this morning.

How was it possible he looked sexier at night? Was it the view from his penthouse? Did he pump some sort of aphrodisiac into the air? I wanted him the moment my eyes glanced his hard body.

"I have thought over our conversation today and I have come to return your gifts," I said, glancing over my shoulder at the packages. "I'll keep the check for the hospital, but you owe me nothing personally. It's too grand of a gesture. We aren't in a relationship, I barely know you actually and I can't keep them. It's inappropriate." I wished he would interrupt me.

"There are no strings attached, Odessa."

"I can't keep them," I repeated.

"If that is how you feel, I understand," he smiled. "Please forgive me if the gesture seemed a bit much. It has been a while since I have wanted to . . ."

"Buy a woman?" I asked, my tone biting and instantly regretting it. "I'm sorry, that was unkind."

"No, it's fair. I told you that it's been a while since I've met a woman who truly inspires me. My delivery was off."

"And last night was a mistake," I said. "I should not have come upstairs with you. My life is my work and I have promised myself that I am going to focus on my job, the very job that you have said inspired you."

"It does inspire me," he said. "You inspire me. There is fire in your soul and seeing you today at the hospital, I realized that even if I only have the memory of our kiss, I am grateful to have met you Odessa Starr."

I swallowed hard and resisted the urge to tell him I felt the same way.

"So, this is it then," Marco said.

"Yes, this is it," I whispered.

We stared at each other. It felt like an emotional showdown. Marco kept his gaze firmly locked with mine, and I wondered which one of us would break first; the trouble was the longer I looked into those deep brown eyes the more I wanted to throw my arms around his neck

"Will you at least sit and have a drink with me?" he asked.

"Probably not a good idea," I said, my voice sounding thinner, breathier to me.

"We can talk about the hospital," he said, holding his hands up. "Tell me more about your work, about your children, about your passions, about what you hate, about your breakfast, whatever you want."

I knew he was grasping at straws, searching for a reason for me to stay. The truth was I didn't want to disappear, not yet. I would return those gifts, but a voice inside my head was insisting that a few minutes with Marco Amador couldn't hurt, right? I needed to stay for the good of the children.

"One drink," I said, stepping towards him.

His face broke into a smile so lovely that I almost reached for his hand.

"Red or white?"

I laughed. “Red, of course.”

“Yes, of course,” he said.

I followed him down a short hall into a big, open kitchen that connected to the living room. The countertops were a glimmering black blue and completely spotless. It looked more like a showroom than an actual kitchen.

“How long have you worked at Children’s?” he asked, uncorking a bottle of red wine that looked and smelled ridiculously expensive.

“I did my residency there and stayed on to do research. I thought I would move east but I stayed on this coast.”

“You don’t like the West Coast,” Eyebrows raised, his poured me a glass of red wine that smelled divine. “It may need to breathe for a moment.”

“No, my family is on the West Coast and I thought I might want some distance. You know how it is, I get one coast you get the other.” I held the glass under my nose and inhaled. It smelled complex with hints of wood and fruit. I felt as though my senses were enhanced beside Marco.

“Ah, distance between family,” he said. “There is a reason I am rarely in Seattle. I get the power of distance.”

Marco leaned against the countertop as he watched me. I was aware of the space between us as I sipped the wine. He was right it was delicious and as we spoke I had the sense that this man was really listening to me.

"Do you get along with your family?" I asked.

"My father is Amador Industries. And Amador Industries is a very big company with many arms. Think of it as a many headed hydra."

"Hydra was a monster," I said, sipping.

"Exactly," he shrugged. "There are monstrous parts of the company and there are good parts. Even the best villains have a redeeming quality right?"

"Well, the funding of the hospital is one of the good parts of your monstrous company then," I said. "You are an interesting man, Mr. Amador," I said.

"Interesting, this is an improvement Ms. Starr," he smiled playfully and using my surname in response. I felt as though we were playing some sort of game; I just didn't know the rules, which made me feel very uncertain. I was used to playing with men, but I was more familiar with setting up the game myself. "So you don't despise me."

"Despise is a strong word," I said, cheeks burning. For a few minutes I'd forgotten about the awkwardness of the night before. The red wine, beautiful room, and conversation had lulled me into a feeling of well-being. "We may not see each other again, but there will be no hard feelings between us. I am not a woman who holds grudges."

“It would be such a tragedy if we didn’t see each other again.”

“I’m afraid I can’t do that.”

“Of course you can,” he said, topping off my glass from the decanter. “You can do whatever you like Ms. Starr.”

“No, this doesn’t work. If I did see you again, I would feel beholden to you.” I said, sipping the red wine. Marco was getting to me, I felt an aching in my core that was undeniable. The way he said my name was formal but so familiar, it turned me on.

“I will never force you to be with me, I will never cage you,” he said. “I can only hope you will change your mind.”

It was early evening and already the darkness of winter had descended upon the skyline. The stars hung outside his windows filling the room with a cool blue light. My mouth went dry as I remembered standing in his bedroom the night before. I felt a bit unsteady on my practical black pumps.

“You look beautiful,” he said. “I’m sorry, I know you didn’t come here to hear that from me, but since you probably won’t be back I may as well tell you.”

“You aren’t going to make this easy on me, are you.” This wasn’t a question.

"Absolutely not," he grinned. "If you leave without my hands on your body tonight I am going to know that I tried everything to get the most beautiful woman I've ever seen into my bed."

"Wow," I said, taking a big gulp of wine.

"You know, I thought you looked beautiful last night, but this is so business like, so proper," he grinned at me and I wanted to know what sexy thoughts were running through his mind as he eyed me from head to toe.

"I do mean business," I whispered.

"And tonight you are here on the business of returning my gifts."

"Exactly."

"I call bullshit," He said.

"You do."

"You could have called me and asked me to pick them up, you could have shipped them back to me, or you could have sent a friend."

"I wanted them out of my apartment right away."

He stepped away from the counter and walked towards me. "You could have boxed them up, thrown a blanket over them, and pretended they don't exist."

"They are lovely pieces I didn't want to damage them."

"So you do appreciate them. I knew you admired fine

things."

I had no words. He had continued to move closer to me with every statement and I hadn't stopped him. Marco was only inches away from me, his fingertips reached out and grazed my arm.

"You are a smart woman Odessa," he said my name slowly as if savoring it.

"Thank you."

"Brilliant, I'd wager."

"I'm just going to say thank you and then go," I said, finally able to break his gaze, I turned and eyed the elevator doors. I just needed to walk towards them.

He traced a fingertip along my arm; I froze in place. I could feel the tingling from his touch extending through my body. I shuddered.

"Do you feel this?" he whispered, placing two fingers against my skin. "I know you think you know me, that you believe I am trying to buy you, to take what I want."

"Or whom you want," I said.

"I get some things," he said. "Other things elude me."

"You poor little rich boy."

"From the moment I saw you last night, I have craved you," he whispered, two fingers replaced by the palm of his hand. His skin against my bare arms, I felt my knees almost buckling as he ran his hands up and down my skin.

"I am not looking for a relationship," I said, wondering why I was telling this man what I wanted at all. I was here to shut a door, why did I feel like I'd opened one instead?

"It doesn't matter what we are looking for," he said. "You and I have found each other. Can we just see where that takes us, can we just be."

He had moved in so close he leaned his forehead down and placed it against mine. His breath near my face, I felt my legs weaken and the wet heat of desire between my legs. I wanted this man, I wanted to feel him inside me, I wanted to wrap my legs around his hard cock and take him inside.

"I came here to return the gifts," I murmured my lips moving closer to his.

"I believe you, stay with me anyway."

"I came here on business."

"I want you, stay with me."

His voice low and sexy, his hands on my skin, my body ached to respond to him and I wondered why not. Marco wasn't asking to put a ring on my finger, why didn't I allow myself this pleasure, this feeling. I hadn't been touched by a man for weeks, and Dr. Mike had been satisfactory but even our hottest nights hadn't made me feel the way Marco did with a single touch.

"Stay with me, Odessa Starr," Marco whispered his mouth against my ear. "Let go, let go and be with me."

"This doesn't mean anything beyond tonight," I said, breathless and dizzy with desire. I wanted to step out of my heels and slide off my pencil skirt.

"Just give me tonight, give us this chance."

I looked up at him, our eyes locking. I reached out and stroked his jaw, pressing my body against his. He moaned slightly and I felt him harden beneath my touch.

"Take me to your bedroom," I said. "Take me in that four poster bed and fuck me until I scream."

In a single move, Marco's arms were around my waist and he picked me up as if I weighed nothing at all.

I locked my arms around his neck and he leaned down and kissed me hard. I moaned and held him tighter feeling the heat between my legs grow wet and hot. Holding me, he strode across the marble floor and into his bedroom throwing me onto the cool sheets of his four poster bed.

CHAPTER 6

My heart raced as my body thrummed with adrenaline and heat; Marco stood above me fully clothed. I lay on the bed in my black skirt and blouse. My eyes never left his face.

I knew what I wanted, I wanted to be naked, and I wanted to rip off my clothes and wrap my legs around his body sliding his hard cock deep inside. I wanted to hear his low voice in my ear telling me exactly what to do. I spent all day being in charge, making life and death decisions, I wanted to give up some of that control.

"What do you want?" I whispered, playing with the buttons above my breasts. "You're in charge Mr. Amador."

"Am I?" he said, his eyes locked on mine eyebrows raised.

"Yes, please Mr. Amador."

"Well then, take off your clothes Ms. Starr, slowly," he said. He took a step away as if signaling to me that he wouldn't come closer until I was done.

I started to unbutton my blouse.

"Wait," he said, "Don't move."

He placed his hands on my hips and ran his palms along the curve of my body down my legs until they reached my feet. He raised one of my feet into the air and tenderly removed my high heel. Then he repeated the gesture with my other leg. I inhaled and shivered at the feeling of his hands on my hips and thighs. He was so close to the places I wanted him, where I needed him and he knew it. "Now you are ready," he said, smiling. "Stand up while you undress."

"Yes, Mr. Amador," I said, standing in the center of the bed.

I pointed to my blouse, the top button.

He nodded and I proceeded to unbutton the blouse exposing a lacy black bra. I undid a few more buttons when he motioned for me to stop. "Wait," he said. "The skirt first, I want to see your pussy."

"Yes, Mr. Amador," I whispered, the thrill of saying his name, of feeling under his control was a stronger aphrodisiac than I expected. I'd never allowed a man to command me like this and it made me feel weak with desire. Standing in my bra with my shirt half undone. I put my hand behind my back and fumbled with the zipper, it kept snagging.

"Turn around," he said, and then I felt his hands on my waist massaging my hip bones. He traced a finger along the waist of my skirt sending shivers through my whole body.

He unzipped my skirt and ran his hands along the cheeks of my ass.

“Take it off,” he said, and I heard him step away.

I started to turn. “Don’t turn around,” he said. “Take it off.”

Facing the wall, my breath coming faster than normal, I shimmied off my pencil skirt dropping it to my ankles and stepping out of it. We had never set any ground rules and I felt as if we were making up our own game as we went along but I loved it. I would wait. Marco would tell me what he wanted, and as long as this ended with his cock sliding deep inside my wet pussy, he could ask me for anything.

“Good,” he said. I could hear the intensity of his breath and wondered how long he’d make me stand here. I didn’t care. Then I heard him move towards me and I felt his hand on my ankle, he ran his hands up the inside of my thigh lingering at the space below my crotch, then he traced a finger up and down my pussy just outside of my panties.

“You wore beautiful underthings Ms. Starr,” he said. I could hear a smile in his face. “This pleases me. Did you wear these for me tonight?”

“The truth Mr. Amador,” I said, staring at the wall, aching to turn around and wrap my arms and legs around him. He played with my panties, running his fingers along the elastic, touching my lips gently with his fingertips.

"Always the truth."

"I love wearing beautiful things," I said, smiling.

"Raise your hands in the air and turn around," Marco said.

I raised my hands and turned slowly wearing my black panties, bra, and white shirt. Marco took my hand and pulled me towards him. "I believe tonight should be about losing control," he whispered. "Before we go further I wanted to ask you if you are all right. Are you enjoying this. We didn't discuss . . ."

"I love it, please fuck me," I said, squeezing his hand and pushing it against my crotch.

"All in good time," he said, pulling his hands away. His hands on my shoulder he pushed the white button down off my body. Then he put his hands under the waistband of my panties and slid them down my legs.

"Spread your legs," he said.

Standing, I spread my legs. Marco leaned forward his mouth on my ankle and moving up the inside of my calf and then to my thigh. He spread my lips apart and ran his tongue in slow circles against my clit. I moaned and felt my legs tremble.

He put his hands on my backside and pressed his face against me harder, his tongue moving faster as I felt an orgasm begin to build. My breathing grew shallow and fast; I softly moaned as I leaned against the heat of his tongue.

"Come for me," he whispered between kisses. "Come for me, I want to taste you when you come."

"I'm going to fall," I gasped, reaching out and putting my hands against his head.

"Come for me Ms. Starr," He said his voice strong with a hint of that temper I'd seen the first night.

Hearing his command pushed me over the edge, I leaned into his tongue and gasped shaking and shuddering as the orgasm shook through my body. Then he was on the bed above me, gently lowering me to the mattress as I whimpered and shook.

"Shhhh, shhhhh," he said, his mouth moving over my neck, my cheeks, and my mouth. I could taste myself, it was acidic and salty and it made me want to be fucked hard.

"You taste like sex," I said, my head rolling back onto the softness of the bed.

"You are sex," he said, his lips against mine. "I need to be inside you."

"Please Mr. Amador."

"Legs together. Hands over your head."

I nodded my body tingling with excitement and need. Marco walked around the side of the bed and reached for my hands extending them over my head, scooting me towards one of the bedposts. With my eyes closed, I could think of nothing but him, his voice, his body, his touch. I felt that I existed for this. My body was made to respond to his voice, to his command, to his call. I no longer cared about keeping my love life uncomplicated; I no longer cared about my failed New Year's resolution the only thing I wanted right then was Marco Amador. Was this love? I didn't know, this was need, this was sex, this was the rawest form of fucking I'd ever experience and I wanted more. He'd tasted me, he'd teased me now I wanted him to fuck me until I couldn't move.

"I want to own you tonight Ms. Starr," he whispered. One of his hands moved up my blouse rubbing against my hardening nipples. "But I'm afraid we have a problem. You are wearing far too many clothes."

"I'm sorry Mr. Amador," I said, reaching for the buttons.

"No, let me," he said grabbing the edge of my blouse. He hesitated and looked at me. "Shall we do this the fast way or the slow way." He grinned wickedly, one eyebrow raised.

"Fast," I said, putting my hand on top of his. "Rip it. Rip it now. Please."

"Good answer," he said, grabbing my blouse and tearing the remaining buttons open. Then his mouth was on mine, and his hand was between my legs pressing softly against my still throbbing pulse. It was almost painful to be so stimulated after coming so quickly. Marco's kisses were electric pulses of energy racing through my body, lighting me up in all the right places. This was the most delicious making out, this was my body aching for more. We pulled apart at last gasping and breathless.

"Sit up," He said, his fingers on the clasp of my bra. He unhooked it with one hand. My breasts exposed he dropped his mouth to my chest his tongue running towards my nipples. He explored each breast with his hands and his tongue sucking and biting with just enough pressure. My head rocked back and I raised my hips up in the air legs spreading. Marco was playing with me perfectly. I was naked and exposed but I didn't feel powerless I felt empowered to let go, to be free, to spread my legs and moan and drip with wetness and please him. In pleasing him, I would be pleased. I wanted to moan for him, to come for him. I needed to be fucked, badly.

"May I ask you a question Mr. Amador?" I asked,

between kisses. I could feel another orgasm building as he caressed my nipples and my clit.

"Yes, you may," he said, grinning. I think he was as pleased as I at how quickly we'd embraced these roles.

"Would you like me to take your clothes off now?"

"Yes, please Ms. Starr." He sat up and stood at the edge of the bed. I moved towards him, running my hands along the waistband of his jeans and slid my fingers up his chest. I stripped off his black turtleneck running my hands along his smooth tan chest and his beautifully inked arm.

We stopped kissing for a moment and I undid the button of his jeans pulling them down over his hips. I got off the bed and turned him around so I could help him step out of each leg.

He stood in front of me wearing black fitted boxers. His erection pushed against the front of his underwear. I took my hand and placed it against his throbbing hardness pressing softly up and down as I stood on tiptoe and kissed him. He responded rocking against my hand and pressing his tongue between my lips. Then my arms were around his lower back and he held me, our lips fused together. For a moment, the games were over. I was no longer his obedient lover, he was no longer my commander, my ruler, we were just ourselves and we were suddenly one. I felt a tremendous warmth through my whole body and a still sense of peace as we stood there entangled our naked bodies pressed together.

I gasped and pulled away for him a moment. His eyes met mine with the same startled look. He stared at me, his eyes narrowing and his lips turning in a sad smile. "I should have met you years ago, you could have changed everything for me," he whispered. "We may not have forever, but I will take as many moments I can get with you Odessa," he said, dropping my surname.

"I don't understand," I whispered kissing him and sliding my hand inside his shorts and grabbing his shaft.

"It doesn't matter," he whispered. "I need you, I need you now."

He lifted me up again and placed me on the bed right in the middle of the mattress. Then he reached into one of the night stands next to the bed. He pulled out a condom and a long black scarf which he held between his hands and snapped it in the air.

I looked at the scarves and the bedposts. I had known this was where we were going the moment I'd met this man and seen his bed, I had hoped for it, I craved it.

"What do you think? He said, nodding towards from the scarf to the bedpost.

"Yes," I gasped. "Yes, please Mr. Amador," I said. Game on.

"Raise your hands up," he said and I obeyed.

My heart racing, he ran his tongue along the inside of my arm and I felt the cool silk of the scarf against my right wrist and a sense of tightening as he secured my arm to the bedpost. He followed by securing the left arm as well.

"Look at you," he whispered, running the palm of his hand across my breasts, my nipples immediately hardening and tingling in response.

I had a brief flicker of doubt. Was I crazy allowing a man I barely knew to tie me to his bed? But I could not escape the feeling that I belonged with Marco. Every cell in my body said yes and I ached to feel him inside me.

I was anchored to each bedpost my legs spread. "Can you move?" Marco asked, as I tugged on the restraints, a surge of adrenaline moved through my body when I felt the containment. I felt trapped but unafraid, I lay before him completely prone.

"I can't move," I whispered breathless and aching for him.

I stared at him as he sat back on his knees between my legs. He sheathed himself with the condom and rubbed my clit in circles then leaned forward taking my nipple into his mouth.

My body tensed with growing pleasure and I spread my legs apart wider as I felt his hips pressing between my legs then the hard tip of his cock pushing against my wetness. I raised my hips up, my arms pulling at the restraints. I wanted to wrap my arms around him but found my movements constrained to my hips and my pussy, it was frustrating and incredibly hot.

Then I felt him pushing inside me, my wetness welcomed him and I felt the sides of my body opening for him, straining and stretching as I took in the enormity of him, he pushed in so deeply that I cried out, arching back.

"Are you okay?" he suddenly asked. "Do you want me to take these off . . ." He reached for the scarves.

"No, no. Don't stop," I said, arching against him again, I felt him move in and out of me, his lips against mine. With one arm above me, he ran his fingers across my clit with the other as he rocked inside me faster and faster. The way he pressed down against my body and pulled out, he was rubbing against my g-spot. I could feel the tightening building inside my body, that telltale buzz that made my eyes blurry. "Oh, please, please, more," I murmured as he rocked in and out of me, faster and faster until I heard him gasp. "Are you ready, are you?"

"Now, now, now," I screamed as an orgasm rippled through me, I felt him push into me and the throbbing pulse of his cock deep inside me as we came together. My body felt satisfied in a way that I'd never felt with any other lover. I lay there shivering and shaking, my body dripping with sweat as Marco pulsed inside of me.

"Odessa Starr," he whispered pulling slowly out of me, I heard him take off the condom and reach for a towel. "How am I ever going to let you out of this bed."

"I have no idea," I whispered, eyes closing. "Well, first you will untie me."

"Right, yes, of course," he laughed, his hands gently untying the knots. "That was fun. And a bit spontaneous. Are you sure you are all right with playing like that?"

"That was an amazing surprise," I said, unable to hide my satisfied smile. I had broken all of my rules and I'd been rewarded with the best sex of my life and I didn't want it to stop. It wasn't just that I wanted Marco right then, I felt as though I needed him. I had never felt a need like this with any lover.

"You know, we could have more fun," he said, lying beside me, his fingers traced down my body, palm resting between my legs. "You realize we need to do that again."

"I know, I know, I know," I said, half laughing as I put

my arm around his chest and rested my head in that wonderful spot between his body and arm. I felt as though he were formed for me, his body shaped to penetrate and hold me like no one else's.

"What is it with this bed anyway," I said, looking at the four posters. "Does it cast a spell on women?"

"Only you Ms. Starr. From now on this bed and my body belong only to you," Marco said, and his mouth was against my lips. I felt him harden and he rolled on top of me, my legs spreading in response.

"That's quite an offer Mr. Amador," I said, as he raised himself up above me and sheathed himself before sliding inside my body.

"For you," he said, his voice lowering and eyes closing. "For you," he said. I cried out as he pushed in and out of me driving me again towards the rawest pleasure I'd ever known.

CHAPTER 7

Morning light filled Marco's bedroom, I awoke to find myself tangled in his sheets, our legs intertwined. Black scarves tied to the posts above our head, clothes draped across thc floor.

The sky outside the pale blue gray of early morning. I glanced at the clock on his night stand and sat up with a start.

The tasteful silver hands on the clock read 8:00 a.m., which meant I had thirty minutes to get dressed, get downtown, and get myself to the hospital in time for the morning staff meeting. It was a Wednesday, and I typically did a read out on the latest patient results which meant I needed at least ten minutes to review the numbers so I didn't look like a bloody idiot in front of the team.

I slipped out of bed, covering myself with one of Marco's beautiful gray sheets. I have no idea why I bothered to cover my skin, I remembered quite clearly he'd tasted and touched almost every inch of my body the night before. We'd had sex three times, twice on the bed, and once on the floor on a pile of blankets. I remembered telling Marco I had to go home a few different times but he had distracted me with his mouth, or had it been his rock hard cock. I remembered wanting to close my eyes for just one minute. Just one minute apparently meant all night.

How had I allowed myself to spend the night? This was so unlike me. I had chosen to have sex with him and lose control in his bedroom but I didn't want that choice to extend to my job.

I rubbed my temples as I found my panties, my skirt and my blouse. I started to button up my blouse realizing there was nothing but torn fabric. The memory of buttons plinking as they bounced on the hardwood floor came to me. Damn Marco and his hot sex. It had seemed like such a good idea at the time especially when I had assumed I'd be going home before heading into the office.

"I'll buy you a new one," Marco said, from the bed.

I turned around to see him propped up on pillows. His chest revealed, I resisted the urge to move towards him and run my fingertips across those perfectly toned muscles, to trace my tongue along the lines of his tattooed sleeve.

"I can buy my own clothes, thank you very much," I said, allowing a grin to escape me.

"Of course you can," he said. "It's a pity to see you with clothes on. I think you're gorgeous of course, but it's a pity." He lifted the sheets revealing more of his toned body and an enormous erection. “Come back to bed, Odessa,” he said.

“I have to work,” I said, resisting the urge to move towards him.

“Call in sick.”

“I take care of children,” I said. “I don’t call in sick.”

“Of course. You’re right. I’m a selfish bastard,” he said, lowering the sheet. “Honestly, I think the work you do is brilliant and meaningful, I envy that.” He closed his eyes.

“Oh come now,” I said, rounding the bed to sit beside him. I allowed myself to reach out and touch the swirling tattoo on his arm. “It can’t be that bad, being the son of a billionaire.” I leaned over and kissed him. “Why don’t you figure out something to do with all of your billions while I’m at work. You poor little rich boy.” I giggled.

“I deserved that,” he said, smiling as he kissed me.

The touch of his lips against mine was electric. I knew this from experience but still the touch of him left me breathless and tingling. He slipped an arm around my waist and pulled me towards him managing to slide my body almost on top of his easily.

“You are a naughty boy,” I said, laughing through our kiss. “I need to go to work and I need to find something suitable to wear so I don't flash my colleagues."

"Don't you just wear scrubs all day?"

"I do wear scrubs, but I also wear normal clothes," I kissed him again, pushing my tongue inside his mouth, he moaned and I felt his grip on my body tighten. "Lucky for you I have a set in my locker. I'll be fine." I glanced at the clock, 8:15 a.m. If there was no traffic, I could be at the hospital in thirty minutes, which would give me a few minutes to change and prep. I would keep my jacket on, it wasn't the worst situation, at least my skirt was still intact. A small miracle.

"Will you come back again, Odessa Starr?" Marco asked me, pulling away. He reached up and held my face in his hands. "I'd like to have dinner with you. Breakfast with you even, I'd like to bury my face between your legs at least once or twice more before you break my heart."

"What makes you think I'll break your heart?" I asked. "You're the one who is supposed to be the heart breaker around here."

He held my face, his thumb stroking my cheek.

"It's rare that I find something or someone in my life that I really truly want," he said. "I want you, you know that."

Marco looked at me with his gorgeous brown eyes.

There was something about his gaze that unsettled me. He looked at me with desire, but there was something more in his eyes, an emotion I couldn't quite put my finger on.

I knew one thing for sure. I had to concentrate to stop myself from reaching out and taking his hand. I wanted to pull him close and promise to never leave him. I wanted to wrap my arms around him and tell him that we'd be together forever.

I froze unsure what to do with these feelings.

"Thank you for last night," I said, leaning down and kissing him. I allowed my lips to linger longer than I should and I felt his hands sliding up my back. "You are going to make me late," I said, slapping his hand away.

"All right, all right. Go to work you amazing woman," Marco said.

Then holding my blouse closed I slipped out his bedroom door.

* * * *

"Good morning," a voice greeted me from the kitchen. I froze holding my blouse closed and my high heels in the other hand.

"Good morning?" I turned to see Veronica sitting at the breakfast bar. Son of a bitch, this was becoming really annoying.

"I'm sorry, I can see I have startled you," she said. She sat at the long black kitchen bar a large porcelain cup of what smelled like herbal tea in front of her. She stirred the liquid with a single silver spoon as she watched me.

"I didn't realize we weren't alone," I said, my pulse racing. I was tempted to yell for Marco but I did not have time for this shit show. "So, do you live here?"

"Sometimes," she said, nodding across the room towards Marco's bedroom. "It's complicated." She wrinkled her nose as if this was a silly little joke.

"I'll bet it is," I said mimicking her nose wrinkle. "How long have you been here?" I asked, bracing myself for her response.

"All night long," she said, in a singsong voice as she stirred her tea.

I thought about all the moaning and screaming and I was instantly incredibly pissed off. How dare Marco allow me to moan and scream without revealing that there was another woman within earshot. And if he hadn't known he should have warned me that another woman *might* be near. I thought about turning around and barging back into his bedroom but I was afraid of providing her yet another show by yelling and screaming. I would not give this gorgeous woman the satisfaction.

"Apologies if I disrupted your sleep," I said. "I was just leaving."

"I'm not his lover," she said. "I'm his colleague. I travel a lot for the business and Marco allows me to stay here when I'm in Seattle. Marco's life is complicated. You should know that before you get any more involved."

"Right, well, whatever, that's wonderful. Good to know," I said, walking to the elevator and pressing the down button. I knew I sounded bitchy but I couldn't help it. What was this cryptic bullshit anyway? Marco didn't seem that complicated. He was a billionaire who was used to getting what he wanted and he had some gorgeous woman who sometimes stayed at his place, and I now had twenty-five minutes to make it downtown to the hospital. I was going to be late. Late, annoyed, and afraid I was already regretting the best sex I had ever had in my whole life. I had promised Marco dinner and more, and once again I was wondering if it was stupid to trust him.

"We should talk more," she said, sipping her tea and shrugging.

"Another time," I said, as the elevator doors opened. I turned and waved, one hand on my blouse; I hoped I looked strong and unaffected instead of rattled and in danger of exposing my sexy bra to a stranger. "Have a great day."

"Cheers."

The elevator doors closed.

Cheers. Damn that was so much cooler than have a great day.

* * * *

Traffic cooperated and I found myself running from the parking lot to the locker room of the hospital, clutching my blouse.

A quick check of my emergency backup clothes revealed the supply I kept on hand for nights with Dr. Mike had not failed me.

I brushed my hair, pulled on a long sleeved black sweater and pants. I shuffled around the bottom of my locker looking for my ballet flats . . . and nothing. I eyeballed my heels. Fine. I never wore heels on the job, but with five minutes to spare this would have to be an exception. I had burned through all my prep time with that awkward conversation with Veronica. I would definitely be talking to Marco about that weirdness. My body wanted him again and my mind was telling me that there was something wrong with this gorgeous employee hanging around his bedroom situation. I was willing to lose control in his bed, but I would not be made a fool by him or any man.

I was three minutes late for the meeting and slipped into the room taking the only open seat right next to Dr. Mike.

"You're late," he said, leaning toward me stating the obvious. He looked well rested and had a green juice on the table in front of him. I assumed he'd biked into work, it was a ten mile ride and something he prided himself on doing daily.

"I overslept," I lied as Marcia Kim displayed the day's agenda. This meeting was for a broader group of doctor's.

"Nice sweater," Dr. Mike said, raising an eyebrow. "Isn't that the one you keep at work?" He asked. I knew what he was asking me, but I ignored it. Why did you use your emergency close stash Odessa? Where were you? Who were you with? Once again, I felt like an idiot for starting an office romance.

"I took that stuff home," I said, taking a sip of coffee and resisting the urge to tell Dr. Mike that what I wore and who I fucked now were none of his business but that would have been disruptive.

"Come on Odessa, you can tell me what is going on," he whispered as Marcia started to recap the hospital financials. "Looks like you had quite a night unless you've decided to start wearing heels to work."

"So nice of you to notice my footwear, I'm trying to listen here, do you mind?" Screw him and his judgments.

I shifted my chair so my back was to Dr. Mike and focused on Marcia just as she summarized the details of Marco's donation. So, Dr. Mike could tell I hadn't slept at home. I hadn't thought about that part of my plan. My backup clothes were known, known to the man I had previously been sleeping with. It was a stupid mistake but it was still none of his damn business what I did.

When Marcia called me to the front of the room to go through the week's study results I just avoided eye contact with him.

"As you can see from the graph," I said, quickly parsing through the curve. "Patients one through ten are all responding very well to the new protocol. We've seen reductions in tumor sizes across all patients. Patient three has shown particular improvements . . ." It was good news, something that distracted me from my worries about Marco and the night before. The new chemotherapy was helping these children live, it was making a difference.

I may not have known exactly what I was doing with Marco Amador, but I knew what my job was the minute I walked through the doors of that hospital. I was there to save lives, to help children fight a bit longer, maybe even beat their cancer into remission.

Besides I didn't know Marco well enough to have real feelings for him. We'd had great sex, that was it. Great sex didn't mean we felt anything but lust for each other, I hardly knew the man. I also wasn't looking for a relationship. I wasn't wired for happily ever after and I didn't want to be.

If that's true, then why did I care a gorgeous woman was drinking tea at his breakfast bar? I really wished that little voice in my head would take a rest.

I buried my conflicting emotions that day diving deep into work. I walked the halls, heel clicking, dodging Dr. Mike's sad eyed stare focusing on my caseload and the patients that we were helping.

"Dr. Starr, these are for you," one of the young candy stripers working the main desk called to me as I was heading to the lab to check on some results. The singsong quality of her voice made me think the news was good at least.

An enormous bouquet of flowers sat on the desk in front of her. There were hydrangeas, roses, and orchids tightly bundled together. It was a gorgeous and ridiculously expensive display of peaches and creams. I loved it, every glorious petal of that over the top flower arrangement.

"Thank you," I said, cheeks burning as I unwrapped the plastic wrap and read the attached card.

Dinner tonight . . . 7:00 p.m.? - Marco. Followed by his number.

The strong lines of his writing made my knees go weak.

"Somebody has an admirer," the young girl behind the desk sang, grinning at me.

I shrugged and smiled, my heart pounding as I picked up the flowers. I turned and almost smacked right into Dr. Mike. He cleared his throat and raised a single eyebrow as he stepped out of my way and walked past.

Once again, I'd managed to unintentionally piss off and probably hurt my ex-lover. I felt badly about Dr. Mike seeing the flowers, they were not the kind of flowers that came from family and Dr. Mike knew enough about my strained relationship with Mom and Dad to know that this was from a different kind of admirer.

I took a moment and rubbed my forehead.

I'd have to talk to him, apologize maybe but for now I had work to do and a choice to make.

After the disastrous run in with Veronica this morning, would I actually see Marco Amador again? My mind said no, but my body said yes, a thousand times yes.

CHAPTER 8

"You like him," Shea said, pouring me a glass of red wine from my kitchen. She had stopped by unannounced after work and was currently camped out at my kitchen table.

"I enjoyed him," I said, taking the glass from her outstretched hand. "There is a difference."

"What does your gut say?" Shea asked taking a seat. Her strawberry blonde hair piled high on her head, she had changed into work out gear for another run.

"My gut says it was fun, really fun, amazing actually." I sighed as I sipped my wine remembering the feeling of his hands against my body.

"None of that sounds bad, you realize that," Shea said.

"Right, but what good can truly come from this. I promised myself to take a break from relationships. It's getting weird at work and I'm afraid Marco has secrets, things he's not telling me. The sex is good, but no sex is that good," I said, lying to myself.

The sex was not just good, it was mind-blowing. My gut told me that the kind of sexual connection I shared with Marco wasn't something to walk away from without a fight. My body wanted to stay. I craved him.

"Marco is complicated," I said. "He is definitely more complicated than Dr. Mike."

"Maybe it's time you did something a bit . . ." Shea hesitated and grinned, "harder." She burst out laughing. "I'm sorry, I'm sorry it was too easy. Harder, you get it?"

"I get it, I get it," I said, laughing. "You are a total goofball, you know that, right?"

"I am the best kind of goofball," Shea said. "And you know I'm right."

"Maybe, maybe not," I said, still smiling. I took another drink and glanced at the clock. I still hadn't responded to Marco's dinner invite. "I'm afraid to trust him. Every time I see him that other woman shows up."

"That is weird, I'll admit that," Shea said. "And he said she works for him, doing what?"

I raised an eyebrow. "You should see her Shea, she is gorgeous."

"So are you."

"I don't trust him," I said, cringing. "I think about all the shit my parents went through. The divorce was awful. My mother is still not functional."

"You can't keep denying yourself happiness based on the past. At least give Marco a chance to explain himself. Don't punish the guy because of something your parents did."

I arched an eyebrow in response. I hated it when people used my personal history against me. "So I trust the guy who has a security detail at his door and a list of woman allowed upstairs."

"First, you said it was a bellboy named Todd and second, did you see this list?"

"No, but there is a book and my name was in it."

"He's a billionaire," Shea said, slowing down for emphasis. "He probably gets wackadoodles trying to get upstairs into his place all the time. For all you know, you are the only woman on the list."

I shrugged remembering Marco's comments that morning about not being used to really wanting someone, the way he had looked at me with those sad brown eyes. I froze. "He seemed sad this morning," I said, remembering his expression. "When we said good-bye he wanted me to stay but he also seemed a little upset. Isn't that strange?"

"Well," Shea said, eyes wide. "He does not seem like some asshole who is trying to use you and toss you aside. Will you just quit being an idiot and ask him about his secrets already? You have nothing to lose. You are always telling me to not over think things, to live my life, enjoy myself, live a little."

"Am I supposed to take my own advice?" I laughed.

"You're the best friend I've got this side of the mountains, and I just want you to be happy," Shea reached across the table and grasped my hand. "You have seen some really sad stuff in your life, you see sad stuff every day. Give yourself some joy. Go, be with this guy again at least so I can live vicariously through you, do it for me, all right? Take one for the team." Shea gave my hand a squeeze before taking the rest of her wine and pouring it into my glass. "You know helping you with your problems is going to interfere with my workout here."

"You should go for your run," I said, standing. I eyeballed the clock 6:00 p.m. I really owed Marco a response.

"Seriously I better run off some of my energy because God knows I don't have anyone to fall into bed with like someone I know." She wiggled her eyebrows at me and winked before heading out the door.

I took a deep breath and stretched as I walked towards my window. This was my life, apartment 304 in The Holiday Apartment building. Outside my window I had a luxury view of the alley and the neighbors run down backyard. It wasn't a $1 million high rise, but it was my home, my space.

I wondered what Marco would think of it.

My body tensed at the idea of allowing him inside my space, my home, my bed. Would he judge me? Would he think it odd that I'd never upgraded after med school? I could afford something fancier but I liked The Holiday. I liked its brick exterior with crawling ivy, I liked the forest green trim and cream colored walls, and I liked the way the hardwood floors shone in the late afternoon. The Holiday had been a dance studio years before, then a boarding house for women only. Rumor had it the place was a brothel once upon a time as well, but I often thought that was just a rumor started by the owner to make the place seem more exotic.

It had seemed impulsive at the time, but I'd lived in this beautiful tidy apartment for almost five years and I had yet to regret a moment here. I also made it a habit to not bring men home with me. Dr. Mike had spent the night with me exactly three times, and every time had felt awkward to me. I always felt he didn't belong with me in this room, inside these four walls.

I stood in the center of my sparely decorated apartment eyeballing my phone. It was 6:15 p.m., I really needed to cancel if I wasn't going to be rude.

My fingers danced across my phone, it would just take

a phrase, a simple dismissal. *Thanks for the flowers and the fun time, don't contact me again. O.*

Or I could postpone the inevitable with something like. *Need time to think. Thanks for the flowers. O.*

The light outside changed quickly the sun disappearing so early in the wintertime, the night sky looked dark, and stars glittered overhead. I was instantly reminded of standing in Marco's condo, our foreheads pressed against the glass. I had felt as though I could extend my fingertips into the sky and touch the stars, to feel their sparkling edges.

My phone beeped.

Pick you up at 6:45? Marco.

I stared at the screen. That was thirty minutes away. If I was going to cancel, the time was now. My fingers poised, I thought about Shea's advice. I could get to know Marco, ask him about Veronica, tell him there could be no secrets between us.

That sounded a lot like a woman looking for a relationship, I thought to myself.

No, it's dinner. Dinner did not mean sex. I was capable of going to dinner with Marco Amador and keeping my clothes on, wasn't I?

It was time to find out.

I'll be ready. O

I hit send. There was no turning back.

CHAPTER 9

The buzzer rang at exactly 6:45 p.m.

"Be right down." I said, my heart pounding. Marco and I were going to have a platonic evening together. At least this was the story I told myself as I gave my outfit a final look in the full-length mirror.

Black skirt and fitted black button down shirt, brown leather boots with knee high stockings with just a touch of thigh showing. To accessorize I wore a single long gold chain. My hair loose and wavy, I wore it pulled away from my face with a black head band. I thought I looked sexy but smart. I didn't want to send Marco the wrong signal, or even worse the right one.

A touch up of my cat's eyeliner and red lipstick. I blotted my lips twice, grabbed my red leather purse and jacket and locked the apartment door.

My heart raced a bit as I walked down the hall. I passed Billie and Bella on the second floor landing. From Billie's red face, it was clear they were in the middle of a lively discussion.

"Madonna. My apartment is haunted," Bella said, hands on her voluptuous hips. Bella lived on the first floor.

We had been neighbors for a short while when she lived upstairs before insisting she needed an apartment with different *energy*. Originally from Venice, Bella was a source of constant entertainment. "There is some tragic unrest between the walls. Tortured souls in my bedroom."

"You can have a séance, but you can't set things on fire," Billie said. "It's not safe." I could all but see her repressing the urge to roll her eyes.

"I just need to burn some of the spirit's old clothes," Bella said. "Set her free."

"Have a good night ladies," I said, smiling as I walked past. Billie and Bella would work it out. Bella is a big believer in the supernatural and must have offered to curse Dr. Mike for me about ten times after our break up. I told her it was unnecessary and to tell the truth, I was a little afraid of what might happen.

I looked out the lobby door and froze.

Marco. He took my breath away.

He stood outside the front door, bathed in a dim light from the single overhead lamp.

He wore another black turtleneck and suit jacket, dark jeans, and what looked like cowboy boots. It was a perfect mix of classy and sexy with just a little bit of wild. I found myself reliving the touch of his bare skin against mine, the taste of his skin. I flushed at the memory and tried to concentrate on my mission. Which was what exactly? Oh yeah, have a nice pleasant evening and decide to trust this outrageously hot man who I feared had the power to steal my heart or break things off with him tonight.

He noticed me standing there and I jumped hoping he hadn't caught me staring.

"Hello," I said, opening the front door.

"Wow," he said, stepping back from me and shaking his head. "You look gorgeous."

"Thank you," I said, feeling turned on already. This staying platonic was going to be more difficult than I thought. What had I gotten myself into?

Marco offered me his arm. "I'm parked in front of the loading zone."

"Sorry there is no doorman," I said, smiling and slipping my arm into his.

"You know I am able to navigate in a world without help sometimes."

"Well, you did manage to track down my address, or did one of your employees do that for you?" I asked, purposely not mentioning Veronica's name. I wanted to see if he would bring her up first, explain her away on his own.

"I looked it up myself, I like to keep my personal

business off my family's radar," he said. "I'm sorry, I should have asked you before invading your privacy like that." He held open the door to the car.

It was a silver BMW, a roadster of some sort. It looked fast and expensive.

"Thank you for the apology." I hesitated before getting into the car. I needed to lay down some ground rules before my libido overruled my common sense. "If I join you for dinner tonight, I will need some more answers from you."

"Absolutely," he said. "I will answer everything."

"And the truth, I always need the truth."

"You mentioned that one before."

"It's a thing with me," I said, shrugging.

Marco stood on the other side of the car door, he reached out and traced his finger along my jaw. "I promise to answer your every question Odessa Starr. I will tell you the truth about myself, the good, the bad, and the ugly and I will never betray you, never." Then he leaned forward and kissed me softly on the lips. My knees almost buckled.

"Well," I said, after his lips left mine, my whole body tingling. "I guess I'm getting in the car now."

"Please do," he said, smiling.

As I sunk into the posh bucket seats Marco walked around the car and climbed into the driver's seat.

He started the engine, at least I thought he did. I noticed immediately that it did not hum like a normal car.

"Electric?" I said, eyebrows raised.

"Saving the planet, any way I can," he winked and put the car into gear.

As we drove, I couldn't help but notice the size of his hand on the gear shift and wish his hands were all over my naked body. I felt dizzy with longing and also from his promise to me. He had agreed to answer my questions and tell me the truth. The question was, did I believe him? Was I really allowing myself to trust a billionaire playboy who was clearly used to taking what he wanted in life?

"I can see the wheels turning in your beautiful head," Marco said, as he turned down 45th heading towards I-5. "You can trust me Odessa," he said. He reached over and briefly squeezed my hand. "I am many things, but I am not a liar, or a stalker."

"Well, you did show up at my work unannounced, you did send me presents unannounced, and you did send me flowers."

"Unannounced." Marco laughed. "Christ, I do sound like a stalker. What are you doing in the car with me? You should get out while you can."

"No way, I've got a list of questions for you," I said,

laughing as well. “You’ve agreed to an interview and that’s what’s going to happen tonight.”

“Sounds sexy,” he said.

“It could be,” I answered in a teasing voice. It was impossible to keep from flirting with this man.

“What is your first question?”

“Easy one to start. Where are we going tonight?”

“I thought that I would make you dinner.”

“At your place?”

“I do have a kitchen, yes.”

“I’m not sleeping with you again,” I said, faster than I intended.

“Understood,” he smiled. “I enjoy your company Odessa in whatever way you feel you want to spend time with me. You want an interview, you get an interview; you want a home cooked meal by me, you get it; you want me to kiss every inch of your naked body, you get it; you want me to fuck you until you beg me to stop, you get that too.”

I inhaled sharply knowing he had made me wet. A single phrase and the man had me dripping for him.

“I see,” I said. my pulse roaring with heat. “You’ll have to give me a minute to decide.”

“In the meantime, lets discuss dinner. This may amaze you, but I cook. I like to cook, my mother taught me. She told me she wasn't going to raise a boy who expected to be waited on hand and foot by the woman he loved."

My body tensed at the word love. I noticed Marco was staring straight ahead now. I looked at his profile, it was so strong, his gaze fixed on the road.

"Your mother sounds like a very smart woman."

"She is, she was," he added. I didn't need to look into his eyes to hear the sadness this time. I could feel it all around him.

I reached out and squeezed his thigh leaving my hand to rest on his leg. "I'm sorry. How old were you when you lost her?" The word died felt too raw, too harsh to me.

"I was just a boy, barely a man, sixteen years old."

Marco turned the roadster onto I-5, hitting the accelerator. We silently raced past the other cars, the BMW's electric motor so quiet it was almost unnerving.

I tried to imagine Marco as a boy saying good-bye to his mother. I remembered how strange it had felt to me in the days after my father left. He hadn't died, but there was loss to process, even if I hadn't realized it at the time. Losing the people you love breaks you into pieces and you have to figure out how to glue yourself back together again and hope you are stronger where you've healed.

I owed it to myself to be strong with Marco. I needed

answers.

"I want to ask you another question," I said, softly. My hand moving up and down his thigh felt so natural. Every touch between us felt electric.

"Anything," he said, glancing my way.

"Who is Veronica really?" I braced myself. "Is she your roommate?"

"My roommate?" he repeated. "No, absolutely not."

"Did she tell you that I ran into her this morning, in your kitchen."

"Christ, no," he exhaled slowly. "She was supposed to arrive after you left. She's helping me with a project that's time sensitive. She should have told me."

"See, that sounds weird to me," I said, unable to stop my pulse from racing. "You aren't really telling me anything about who she is, project, time sensitive. Those are just words."

Marco put his hand over mine. "You have to trust me. There is nothing romantic between us. Veronica is like a sister to me."

"She's beautiful, she's charming," I said.

"She is all those things and I love her as if she is family," he said, emphasizing the last word.

"You should have told me she'd be at your place. She

probably heard me crying out in ecstasy last night."

"Ecstasy?" he said, grinning. "I'm glad to know we feel the same about our night together."

I took a breath and let the knowledge that he'd enjoyed our night together as much as me sink in for a moment.

"I apologize for this morning," Marco said, his voice grew serious. "I would never intentionally embarrass you."

"That's good to know," I said.

"Veronica is the daughter of my mother's best friend."

"And she lives with you?"

"She stays with me sometimes. Veronica works for the government," he said. "She works for an agency that requires her to go undercover which means she has a home of her own in San Francisco, but she is rarely there."

"I feel silly asking this, but is she a spy?"

"She is not a spy. She works on drug cases, the DEA."

"And you two are just friends."

"I grew up with her. As a boy before my mother died, we lived half the year in Guadalajara, the other in New York City. Veronica was my first friend in the United States. She has been a good friend to me through the years. She and her family were a tremendous support to me when Mom died. She has never and she never will be my lover. Do you believe me?"

The car idled at a stoplight downtown. He turned to face me and I studied his expression as he held my gaze steady. A single word kept running through my mind. Yes. Say yes to this man.

I couldn't breathe in the silence between us. I felt as though this moment had meaning, that my fate hung on this one question. Did I believe him? Would I let go of my fear and let my heart choose my future instead of my mind?

"What do you say Odessa. Do you believe me?" Marco asked again, his voice just above a whisper.

"I do," I said, a feeling of intense joy and freedom moving through my body. "Yes, I do." The double meaning of my words were not lost on me, and for once I didn't back pedal and pull them back.

Marco grasped my face between his hands and kissed me sending shivers through my whole body. Our lips pressed together I felt as though we were sealing a bond, an agreement between our souls binding us together.

The spell was broken by a honking horn behind us.

"Lights changed," I gasped looking at the green light overhead.

"All right, all right," Marco said, turning back to the wheel. "You have got me so distracted."

"Is that a bad thing?" I asked, running my hand up his

thigh and moving it across the crotch of his pants. I felt him instantly respond growing hard with my touch.

“No, not a bad thing,” he said. “I want to get you upstairs. Quickly.”

“Drive faster then,” I said, pressing my hand against the hardness between his legs.

* * * *

Inside the hotel, Todd the bellman was standing guard by Marco’s private elevator.

“Mr. Amador,” he said, his eyes growing wide as we approached. “Good evening, Ms. Starr, welcome back Ma’am, I mean Miss.”

Marco leaned over to Todd and whispered something as he handed him his silver keys.

“Of course sir,” Todd said. He pressed the up button and then immediately walked away.

“What did you say to him?” I asked, as the elevator doors opened.

“I asked for some privacy.” Marco turned to face me as the doors closed.

I threw my arms around him as he lifted me and pressed me up against the elevator wall. His tongue in my mouth, my legs wrapped around his waist. I felt his hand slide up my skirt and inside my panties. He parted my lips with his fingers and slid deep inside as he rocked against me.

"More," I gasped as his fingers slid in faster and faster. The elevator flying skyward I felt that familiar heat start to build in my core. The elevator chimed as we hit the top floor and the doors opened.

Marco slid his fingers out and carried me across the entry way, his lips against mine still. He threw me down on the couch where we had talked that very first night and hiked my skirt up over my hips. Then before I could say a word his lips were between my legs. His tongue moving in circles with just the right amount of pressure.

I moaned and leaned my head back grasping his head with my hands pushing him against me even harder. He brought me to the edge of coming faster than I thought possible. And then suddenly I felt that unfurling feeling as my body shook and shuddered against his lips, pleasure rippling through me like an enormous wave.

I looked up and Marco kissed me on my lips, his hands discretely pulling my skirt back down over my hips. "Now, that's better, isn't it," he smiled.

"I don't think I can stand now," I said, laughing. "This may be a problem."

"You don't need to," he said, brushing a hair off my

forehead. "You can just stay here and be gorgeous while I slave for you in the kitchen. As long as you are here with me, it's all I need," he said.

* * * *

Marco's dining room table was set for two with simple white plates and crystal glasses. In the kitchen I heard him chopping what I assumed were vegetables and the sound of meat sizzling. Soon the condo was filled with the aromas of sweet and hot spices.

I noticed a fire lit in the lovely fireplace in the sunken living room, the stars outside were just as bright as I remembered. The sky looked black and cold, the twinkling lights standing out like flickering white flames. There was such beauty here, it was ethereal, seductive, impossible to resist.

After my legs had recovered, I moved to the kitchen and sat at the bar to watch him cook.

He smiled and pushed a wine glass towards me. "Did you come to check up on me?"

"I wanted to make sure it was really you chopping up a storm in here. You sure you don't have a cook hiding somewhere?"

"Nope, it's just me," he said, stirring an enormous cast iron skillet filled with peppers, onions and grilled chicken.

"Do you cook often, or only when you're trying to seduce a woman?"

"First, I don't cook to seduce women," he said, shaking the skillet and turning his attention to a small bubbling pot of red sauce. He tasted it and added some additional spice. "You are the first woman I have ever shared Mama's enchilada recipe with."

"Are you serious?" I said, taking a big gulp of wine.

"I told you, nothing but the truth."

"So do you cook for yourself then?"

"I do, but it's more fun to share it with someone. I don't eat out a lot. I can't."

"What do you mean?"

"If I go to a restaurant on my own, I end up in a gossip column with a photo of the depressed and destructive Amador son, doomed to break the rules and his father's heart."

"You are serious."

"Absolutely," he smiled. "I can tell you don't troll the internet for other people's misery. Please don't google me."

"I don't read gossip online," I said. "I'm not above gossip, there is just no time in my life."

"If I took you to a restaurant tonight for example, we'd end up on someone's phone, then online, and next my family would become interested in you."

"So you are hiding me from your family?" I asked, half asking as a joke.

Marco looked at me all traces of a smile vanishing from his face. "My family is complicated," Marco said. "I want to spare you from scrutiny. I would do anything to keep you safe."

"So serious," I said. "We are just friends having dinner."

"I think we are more than friends, Odessa," he said, his eyes locking with mine. He walked around the counter and stood between my legs hiking my skirt up a bit so he could lean into me. Then he tilted my chin up slightly with his hand. "I've learned that it's impossible to predict how much time we have with the people we love in this life. I can tell you that I want as many nights as I can get with you."

"Do you say that to all the girls," I whispered aching to be kissed.

"I say that to none of the girls," he said. "And I think you believe me." He leaned forward and inhaled as he breathed in my hair his lips finding my jaw. Then I was on my feet, our lips locked together.

His kiss rippled through my body, starting with my

lips. I felt myself dripping wet again. I ached to feel him inside of me. It was as if Marco Amador had found the controls to my body and soul. One soft kiss and I melted. Who was I standing next to this man? I certainly felt outside of myself.

"Is it time for dinner?" I said, trying to sound light and easy but instantly thinking of nothing but getting naked. The bed was just around the corner, down a short hallway, a simple left and then a right. All it would take would be a phrase, a few words, a simple statement. I glanced down the hallway and then into the kitchen.

"What's wrong?" he said, eyebrow raising. "You look . . . undecided."

"I am," I said, leaning into him and running my finger along the line of his tattoo up his neck. Don't resist him, a voice whispered inside my head. Taste him. Make him yours. He already is. "I'm just not sure if we should eat dinner before or after."

Marco looked confused for a moment then his eyes widened and a slow smile crossed his face. "I am," he said, eyes wide a slow smile crossing his face

Then he picked me up off the ground as if I weighed nothing, holding me in his arms like a bride about to cross the threshold with her beloved. My arms locked around to neck, I held on as he walked me across the room stopping just outside his bedroom door.

"I am going to make love to you and then I will feed you some kick ass enchiladas and an arugula salad with fresh oranges, followed by a crème brûlée that I torch myself."

I laughed between kisses. "Love me and then feed me, but please take me to bed, take me now."

"You will never need to ask me twice woman," and he walked me through the door throwing me onto the silky sheets of his four poster bed.

CHAPTER 10

The shades were drawn in the bedroom. As I lay on the bed, Marco walked to the enormous glass windows and hit a button on the wall. The blackout shades rose with a soft humming noise revealing the brutally clear night sky. Stars hung outside the glass like sparkling pendants, the city lights reflected on the black water of Puget Sound and across the waves the distant lights of Bainbridge Island glimmered. It was silent and ethereal.

"It's so beautiful," I said, propping myself up on my elbows and drinking in the view. "It's solitary but it doesn't feel lonely."

"It used to feel lonely," he said, turning to face me. "Before you."

He could take my breath away with a few words and a look. My heart pounded with desire and fear of how much I wanted this man.

"Nothing makes me happier than seeing you in my bed Ms. Starr," he said, his voice low. My body tensed with anticipation at the sound of my proper name. I liked this little game, I couldn't wait to relinquish some control to this beautiful man. "Do you like pleasing me?" He asked.

"Yes," I whispered. "I'd like to please you more Mr. Amador."

He raised a finger and ran it up and down the buttons of my blouse. "Undress for me," he said softly pointing to the window. "Stand in the moonlight."

"Yes, Mr. Amador," I said. I slid off the bed and moved towards the window before turning and slowly unbuttoning my blouse. I dropped it to the floor and then slipped out of my skirt standing in nothing but my bra, panties, boots, and stockings.

"Take off everything," he said.

I nodded and unzipped my boots sliding them off my legs and then rolled my stockings off one at a time. I unhooked my bra exposing my breasts. I felt my nipples go hard in the cool air and then I slipped off my panties dropping them onto the floor.

He walked towards me and breathing slowly ran his hands over my skin, my whole body tingling from his touch. He reached up and removed my black headband before running his fingers through my hair.

"I have never seen anyone so beautiful," he said, softly walking in a slow circle around me, his fingertips tracing a line across my skin.

I closed my eyes and exhaled softly enjoying this

feeling of being worshipped. I enjoyed being naked in front of him. I felt vulnerable and exposed and incredibly turned on. His hands found my lower back pulling me closer, his mouth found mine and his tongue was inside my mouth; my body ached for more of him, pressing against him I moaned.

He stepped away from me and pulled his turtleneck off exposing his cut chest and the tattooed sleeve. Then he took my hands placed them on his belt buckle and nodded.

I undid the silver buckle and the button to his pants then dropped to my knees as I slid his jeans off his body one leg at a time.

I placed my hand against the bulge in his black briefs. He inhaled and nodded. My breath grew shallow with anticipation. I lowered his shorts exposing his enormous cock and took him in my mouth.

He placed his hand behind my head as I moved him back and forth rolling my tongue over his ridges, playing with his sensitive tip. I wanted to bring him pleasure, I wanted to know I had the power to make him come with my mouth.

"Easy," Marco said, stopping me and taking my hand he helped me to my feet and led me to the bed. He lay down on the sheets and pulled me on top of him our legs intertwined, lips locked in a long slow kiss.

"The condoms," I whispered.

"Open the drawer," he said. "There is a surprise for you inside."

"For me?" I said, eyebrows raised. "You knew we'd end up in bed?"

"I hoped," he said, grinning.

I straddled him, my wet pussy resting just above his throbbing cock. I reached into the night stand drawer, quickly finding the pack of condoms and noticing a small black box with a thick red ribbon. I pulled out the box.

"Open it," he said, smiling.

My legs wrapped around his waist as I undid the ribbon and opened the box. Wrapped in red tissue paper was a round silver disk with a silicon nub that ran like a ridge across the middle.

"My my," I said, smiling and holding the very discrete vibrator. I had used a vibrator before, but never on a regular basis and I had never actually incorporated toys into playtime with a lover. My pulse raced with anticipation, apparently I liked the idea.

"Would you like to try it?" he asked, sitting up a bit.

"Yes, I think so." I felt suddenly very nervous.

"Let me show you."

I nodded and handed him the silver disk. He flipped a flat switch and I heard a low buzzing. While I straddled him he took the vibrating disk and placed it against my clit. The rush of pleasure was instantaneous. I rocked backward but he held my lower back so he could keep the pressure on.

"Grab the condom," he said, nodding towards the wrapper moving the vibrating disk away. "Don't worry, we aren't done playing," he said, smiling.

I unwrapped the condom and sheathed him quickly. Then I raised my body up and lifted his heavy cock sliding him inside me. I gasped again at the size of him, my body straining to take him in, but the wetness inside of me opening me up.

I leaned forward over him my breasts hanging down as I moved up and down, every time he slid into me I gasped with pleasure.

He moaned and reached for me, his fingers finding my nipples, he grasped one of my breasts in his hand and twisted the nipple as I pushed against him. It was a sharp feeling, the pleasure and pain mixing together in a way I had never experienced. I moaned as I drove down onto his enormous cock. I felt as though there was nothing in the world but our two bodies connecting, he was inside of me, filling me up, sliding deep into my core.

Then I felt his hand against my pussy and heard the sound of the vibrator just as he placed it against me with a deep thrust. He had changed the setting so the device vibrated at a lower intensity and then increased and repeated creating a wave of pleasure.

I felt Marco push into me harder and deeper as the vibration against my pussy increased. I don't remember moaning, I don't remember anything but the feeling of his cock inside me of and my clit aching with need.

Our breathing heavy and ragged. I don't remember speaking, I don't think I could form words, but there was no reason to ask for more. Marco could feel me, we were moving as one connected body, fucking each other in perfect timing until the heat between us spilled over and I felt myself unraveling around him. I cried out as he thrust into me one final time, my whole body shaking and shuddering with the vibrator against my pussy and his throbbing cock inside me. I had never had such an intense orgasm in my life. I felt as though the stars outside his window had filled our room with light, my senses were on high, my whole body pulsing and alert with pleasure.

I rolled off of Marco and lay beside him shaking.

We said nothing for a few minutes. We just lay there

on the bed our bodies shaking.

Then Marco rolled over onto his side and traced his fingers along my body.

"This," he said, leaning forward to kiss my forehead.

"This?"

"I have been dreaming of feeling like this with a woman my whole life."

"You are not what I expected Mr. Amador," I said, smiling. I ran my hands down the stubble of his cheek.

"And what were you expecting?"

I rolled onto my back and looked at the ceiling. "Oh, I don't know. A spoiled man child who couldn't take care of himself."

"And you haven't even tried my enchiladas yet," he said, laughing and kissing me on the lips. "Shall we dine?" he said propping himself up on one elbow.

"Yes, please, I'm famished."

He kissed me one more time and hopped out of bed giving me a glorious view of his ass as he walked across his bedroom to what appeared to be a walk in closet. He returned wrapped in a thick black robe and handed me a soft white one with the hotel's monogram on the pocket.

"Fancy schmantzy," I said, giggling as I jumped out of bed and wrapped myself in the soft robe.

Marco offered me his hand and I followed him out of the bedroom. In that moment, I had no regrets about Marco Amador outside of having to leave the warmth of his bed. I foolishly believed that I could make love to that man, body and soul, and keep my heart under lock and key. I told myself it was a physical connection, a release of endorphins that made me hold his hand so tight as we walked hand in hand across the room, but the truth was I had fallen in love with him the first time we kissed.

I couldn't admit it to myself at the time, but I knew I couldn't stop touching him. I decided that I needed to make things work that Marco Amador. I had no idea how hard that would be.

CHAPTER 11

Marco and I sat next to each other at his long dining room table. He set the places side by side so we weren't replaying some medieval scene with miles of table between us. In fact, he kept reaching under the table and rubbing my knee between bites of his enchiladas.

"Your mother taught you well," I said, taking my last bite of the dish. I was officially full. The spices had just the right amount of bite, the chicken was tender and perfectly charbroiled and the vegetables just crispy enough. "You ever want to quit your day you could open up one of those trendy lunch trucks."

Marco's face lit up. "You know my mother and I used to talk about opening a restaurant together," he said. "It was silly really, but something we shared. She was a wonderful cook." He smiled as if he were replaying a memory in his mind. "She used to take me into the kitchen with her and I'd be her assistant, cutting vegetables, making sauces. I loved it. I always knew I was lucky."

"That is so sweet," I said, taking a sip of red wine. "Why haven't you done it without her?"

"She was the talent," he said, sighing and leaning back

in his chair. “The point was she inspired me to dream, to want more than just work in the family business. It drove my father crazy the way she parented me. He wanted her to hire a nanny, a cook, a chauffeur when we lived in Guadalajara, but she insisted on spending time with me. I remember my father actually hired a nanny once and my mother fired her on the spot.” He smiled. “I loved how she stood up to him. I remember it still.”

I thought of my mother and the way she had crumbled without my father, the opposite of strong. I wished I had been raised by a woman like Marco’s mother, and I instantly felt guilty for thinking such a horrible thought.

“My mother always told me that the most important thing in life is to remember who you are, where you came from. My family wasn’t always rich. Before my father founded the import export business, my parents were from poor families. My mother never forgot who she was. She was always grateful.”

“And your father?” I asked looking at Marco over the top of my wine glass.

His eyes met mine, the coldness in his gaze gave me my answer.

Marco poured me another glass of wine. I felt blissfully sleepy, relaxed but not drifting. My body felt thoroughly exhausted but the dinner had given me some energy. I wasn't falling asleep at the table yet.

"The service here is wonderful," I murmured, reaching up to stroke his cheek as he leaned over me.

"Well, the clientele is intoxicating," Marco said, kissing me.

I was exhausted but every kiss from this man made me want to drop my panties.

"Odessa is an unusual name," Marco said when we'd taken a breath. He reached over and interlaced his fingers with mine, his skin felt warm against mine.

"It's Ukrainian," I said, unable to stifle a yawn. "A city actually in Ukraine. My mother was born there. It seems she's a bit sentimental. And stuck in the past, and totally dysfunctional and unable to do anything on her own."

"And you are so driven."

"Ah yes," I took another sip of wine. "My response to her low functioning life style is to be a high functioning type A personality. At least that is what I've been told."

"Told by who"

"Ex-boyfriends, family members, it doesn't matter really," I rolled my eyes remembering one of Dr. Mike's rants about my emotional unavailability. "The fact is my parents split. My mother is Ukrainian, my father was . . . is from Minnesota. He's a dentist. They met when my mother moved here when she was eighteen." I sighed. "Boy meets foreign girl, boy and foreign girl fall in love. Boy grows up and gets bored, abandons his family while foreign girl loses her marbles. It's a classic rom-com."

"Do you talk to your father?"

"Not if I can help it," I said, giving a falsely bright smile. "He has a new family. It's an old story, nothing new. I don't want to bore you with it."

"You aren't boring me. It's incredibly sad."

"It's not sad, it's just something that happens. I'm over it. And it's not my dad's betrayal that is the sad part, it's how my mother fell apart. She fell the fuck apart. With no means, no motivation. Dad has been gone for eighteen years and she still thinks he's coming back . . .eighteen years."

"Is it that bad to never stop believing in the person you love?" Marco said, standing and taking my place. "She must have really loved him."

His comments stunned me for a moment.

"Yeah, she did, I think she really did," I said, watching him walk into the kitchen. Marco was right, my mother had been in love, so in love that she lost herself completely. A mistake I didn't want to repeat.

Marco walked back into the room and offered me his hand. “Are you ready for dessert?” His smile was ridiculously suggestive.

“I can’t, I want you, but I don’t think I can come another . . .”

“Shhhhh,” he helped me to my feet and holding my hand led me across the room. “I thought we might do something very unique this time, very special.”

“It sounds exhausting,” I said, softly as we walked into his bedroom.

Marco led me towards the bed. “I want to crawl into that bed and do one thing with you Odessa Starr, and one thing only.”

“You do?” I asked weakly.

“I want you to fall asleep in my arms,” he said, smiling.

“Oh thank God,” I said, laughing. I threw my arms around him and rested my head against his chest. “Then take me to bed or lose me forever. I don’t think I can stand another moment. You’ve wrecked me.”

Marco laughed and lifted me up slipping me out of the soft robe. I slid beneath his sheets and closed my eyes.

CHAPTER 12

"Hello, Ms. Starr," Todd the bellman now made it a habit to greet me at the garage when I arrived at the hotel. It was equal parts charming and unnerving. "Your bag?"

"Thanks Todd," I handed him my overnight bag and followed him up a staircase that led from the top floor of the garage to the lobby. "So, do you just hang out here in the garage waiting for me?" I asked him as we walked up the stairs. "How do you know when I'm arriving?" Once Marco had given me a parking pass, Todd had mysteriously been appearing whenever I parked my car. My own personal escort. It was a bit strange but I had to admit I was happy to have the help with the bags I carted back and forth from my house to work and to Marco's every day.

"Mr. Amador has strict instructions that you are to be escorted upstairs," Todd said, leading me around a small corner right to the private elevator that led to the penthouse.

"And you just wait for hours then?" I looked at my watch, it was 10:00 p.m. "I was late tonight, over an hour. Don't you have other guests you are supposed to help?"

"I work exclusively for Mr. Amador now," Todd said, rocking back on his feet a proud grin on his face. Then the elevator doors opened and his face fell as if he had just remembered something. "I probably shouldn't have told you that," he said.

He cringed and hit the button that led to Marco's penthouse. "Please don't tell Mr. Amador. I signed an NDA and he pays so much better than the hotel."

"Don't worry, I won't out you to the boss." Marco hadn't mentioned to me that Todd was on his staff. It didn't feel like a betrayal it was just interesting. I figured he had a bit more experience than me hiding from paparazzi and navigating this gossip riddled world as a billionaire.

The doors opened. Todd nodded and placed my bag in the entry way.

"Anything else ma'am?" He asked.

"Yes," I smiled. "Can you please call me miss? You make me feel like an old lady with all this ma'am stuff."

"Yes, ma'am . . . I mean miss." Todd's freckled cheeks flushed. "I'll be downstairs if you need anything. And thank you about . . . you know."

"Of course, Todd," I said, turning at the sound of voices in the condo. Marco was having an animated conversation with a dark haired man who appeared to be adjusting the branches of what looked like a sculpture of a large silver tree. A beautiful red haired woman sat on the couch by the fireplace turning pages in a catalog as if she were waiting for an appointment.

"Hello," I said, walking into the room, worried I should have called before arriving. "Sorry to interrupt."

"You're not." Marco's face lit up when he saw me. He strode across the room and planted a long lingering kiss on my lips. "Hello gorgeous," he said, taking a moment to look into my eyes.

"Hello," I giggled a little embarrassed at his display of affection.

"Theo Manhattan, this is Odessa Starr," Marco held my arm and called over his shoulder to the man by the tree.

Theo stopped his work and nodded at me. He had long wavy dark hair and the palest blue eyes I'd ever seen. "It's a pleasure to meet you," he said with a lilting British accent. "I apologize for interrupting your evening, this bloody installation was supposed to take an hour."

"Installation?" I said, as Marco took my hand and led me around the couch so I could sit beside the red haired woman.

"I'm Grace," she said, softly extending her pale hand. "I'm with Theo. I'm here for emotional support only." She nodded at the man beside the tree catching his eye. He stopped his work to smile at her. It was clear in that moment that they were deeply in love.

"Theo is the artist I told you about," Marco said.

"You made the bird cages," I said, the pieces falling into place. "Marco is a great admirer of your work."

"She gifted them back to me," Marco said, to Theo his lips in a tight line of mock anger. "I gave them to her and she just sent them back as if they were nothing at all. She may be beautiful, but no doubt about it, she's cruel. Cruel I tell you."

"Come on," I said, laughing. "It was too much. They were lovely Theo, really they were. You are very talented."

"You don't need to apologize to me," Theo said, stepping back from the sculpture. The trunk of the tree stopped at about six feet with the branches extending even higher.

"I'll help," Grace said, standing. "It's beautiful babe, it really is." Grace got up off the couch and picked up one of the birdcages from the auction hanging it on a thin branch. Marco offered me his hand and we stood together as Theo and Grace arranged the cages on the tree in front of the enormous glass window that faced the night sky.

"Now that's complete," Theo said, stepping back from his work. Grace sidled up beside him slipping her hand into his. The two of them made quite a pair with his blue eyes and her dark red hair and pale skin. She reminded me of a woodland fairy, ethereal and sparkling, yet something about her gaze suggested a fire burned in her soul. I liked her. I liked him. I could see why Marco had invested so much time in this artist and in his art.

"I love it," Marco said, walking to the sculpture and tracing his fingers over the branches. "Now aren't you sad you gave me back those cages, Odessa?" he joked.

"I don't have room in my studio for a display like this," I said.

"Right then, we'll be off." Theo said. He packed up a small tool chest with Grace's help and the two of them walked hand in hand to the elevator. "It was lovely meeting you Odessa, good night." The elevator chimed and Theo and Grace disappeared downstairs.

Marco slipped behind me and wrapped his arms around my waist leaning down to whisper in my ear. "Do you like the sculpture?"

"Yes," I said, admiring the way the light hit the branches and the cages. It was such a clever way to display the birds. "It's gorgeous, so modern."

"I have a gift for you," he said.

I tensed up looking at the tree. "Not the cages, I've told you it's too generous."

"And I listened," he said. "This is a different kind of gift, something that I think you will consider more reasonable." His lips against my ear he gave me a soft kiss sending chills through my body. "Follow me," he whispered, leading me across the room.

"You know I don't want anything from you," I said, as we walked into his bedroom.

"You don't?" He turned and smiled at me, one eyebrow arched.

"Well, there is something I do want from you actually," I said, placing my hand right on the bulge in his pants. I felt him harden at my touch.

I moved to kiss Marco when he pointed to the bed.

Sitting on the edge of the mattress was a blue toothbrush boxed up and tied with a crisp red ribbon.

My eyes widened. "A toothbrush?"

He nodded and picked it up handing it to me then dropping to one knee.

"Stop it," I said, laughing nervously shocked at the rush of emotion I felt at seeing that man on bended knee.

"Odessa Starr," he said, with reverence. "Will you take this toothbrush and keep it in my bathroom as a sign of your commitment to fuck my brains out every night if you so choose." He looked up at me grinning.

"You are ridiculous," I laughed, pulling him to his feet. "Stand up, come on."

"It's time," he said, reaching for the toothbrush and handing it me. "I want you to know that you belong here, to not worry about packing up all your belongings and disappearing in the morning light."

I stood in front of him my mouth dry. He had a point. Hauling my things back and forth was becoming more of a chore and I constantly worried I'd screw up again and end up walking the hospital halls in slutty red heels.

"I told you the night I met you that I don't believe in cages, but I want you to know that you have a place with me." Marco nodded towards the closet. "You'll find an empty rack inside if you so choose to bring a few things here."

My eyes darted from the toothbrush to the closet to Marco to the bed. Heart racing I took a breath. My normal play was to cut and run but here I stood not speaking and not taking a step away.

"I've freaked you out," he said, cringing. He brushed a hair off my forehead. "You have to speak, say something. I've turned you into a mute."

"I'll take the toothbrush," I blurted throwing my arms around his neck and kissing him as a rush of adrenaline raced through my body.

He laughed kissing and undressing me with every stumbling step we took towards that bed. “Stay with me,” he said when we’d fallen onto those gorgeous gray sheets. He stopped kissing me and gazed directly into my eyes with a seriousness that surprised me. “Promise me you’ll stay with me as long as you can.”

“I don’t expect to go anywhere,” I said. “Are you?”

He answered me with a kiss and within moments I’d forgotten that he’d never really given me an answer.

CHAPTER 13

The next night Todd did not meet me in the garage. I took the back staircase and was about to head up the private elevator when Veronica intercepted me placing her hand on the up button.

"Veronica. Hi?" I said, my finger poised awkwardly close to her skin.

"We need to move," she said, taking my arm and pulling me away from the doors. "Quickly."

"Excuse me?" I said, stumbling a bit as she led me around the corner and past the front desk. With every step I became more confused and irritated. I hadn't seen Veronica in weeks and here she was dragging me around the hotel as if I were a piece of property.

"I'll explain," she said, walking me across the lobby into a small bar that faced First Avenue. The walls black, blue neon accents lit the walls. A woman stood at a small stage in the back of the room crooning out a sad sounding jazz tune.

Veronica slipped into a booth and directed me to sit across from her.

I stood at the edge of the table, my heart pounding.

"No," I said, feeling dizzy with rage. "I'm not doing anything until you tell me what is going on. Where is Marco?"

"Please sit," she said. "We don't need a scene."

"Tell me and I'll sit."

"You can't go upstairs, not now," she said, rubbing her forehead. "For Christ sake Odessa, Marco sent me downstairs to keep you safe. Sit. The. Fuck. Down."

Her words stunned me into silence. I sunk into the booth.

"What's going on?" I said, a feeling of dread creeping into my belly. Suddenly Todd's nightly escorts didn't seem to meaningless, the private elevator and back staircase now took on an ominous tone. "Who is he hiding from up there?" I asked.

"Marco doesn't hide," she looked at me as if she pitied me. "I'm here to protect you, not him."

"Enough with the cryptic bullshit Veronica," I said, leaning across the table. "I know you have some sort of special relationship with Marco, but so do I. Tell me what is going on, I don't deal well with ambiguity."

"Marco's father has come to town," Veronica said, again rubbing her temples. "Luis is here. He is upstairs."

"So, what?" I said. I felt like my brain was on over

drive trying to put together a puzzle filled with missing pieces.

"Why do you think Marco hides out in the penthouse in Seattle? The Amador family runs their business out of New York, Seville, London, and Guadalajara. Yet, Marco chooses to mold in the rain and the cold."

"I thought the Amador foundation was based here."

"No, the foundation has fundraisers all over the country. The night of the New Year's Eve bash for Children's there were six other parties across the world." She wrinkled her brow. "You really didn't google him did you?"

"No," I said, flushing with embarrassment. "He asked me not to."

"Christ, you are something else," Veronica said. Her dark brown eyes looked weary and she had circles under her eyes. "Would you like a cocktail? Something strong perhaps?"

"Yes. Fine," I said, my mind still spinning.

Veronica got up and went to the bar to order. I felt grateful for the darkness of the bar. I closed my eyes and inhaled and exhaled slowly. I needed to calm my racing heart. Had I trusted Marco too soon? Family secrets were one thing my mind reasoned, just because the man hadn't told me more about his father didn't mean he would betray me.

Marco had promised me total honesty and here I was being squirreled away as if I were an untouchable.

Veronica returned holding two low ball drinks. "Whisky," she said.

"Nice," I took the drink.

"Don't worry it goes down smooth."

"That's a relief." I took a sip of the drink and allowed the heat to move through my body. It gave me a moment to really look at Veronica. She was still gorgeous, all legs, lanky but muscular and strong. She wore a short sequined skirt and a yellow cashmere sweater that popped against her deep brown skin. Her brown hair cropped close to her skull she had amazing bone structure. She looked as though she'd just finished walking the runway at fashion week.

"Marco says you work for the DEA," I said, taking another sip of my whisky. "Is that true? You don't really look like a government employee you know."

She widened her eyes and took a sip of whiskey. "Looks can be deceiving."

"Whatever, I'm done here," I said, moving to slide out of the table. Veronica dropped her arm across the table grabbing my wrist.

"Let's just get this out into the open," she said. "Marco is like a brother to me. I have never seen his dick."

"I wasn't asking about his dick," I said, trying to act shocked. I had been wondering. Damn. I thought I was better at hiding my insecurities.

"Yes, you were," she laughed, letting go of my wrist. "You can pretend to be coy, when really what you are wondering is if the man has taken his dick anywhere near me. Have I known his touch? Has he tasted me? Have I ever fucked your man?"

I laughed trying to cover up how well she'd seen through me. "He's not my man."

"Bullshit," Veronica said. "I have known Marco since we were both eight years old. The boy is a man now and he does not love many. But he loves you." Veronica smiled at me and sipped her whiskey.

"He loves me," I repeated downing the rest of my drink. Her words stunned me. Was it true? Of course it was true. I didn't need Veronica to tell me, I could feel it in his touch in the way he loved my body every night. "Why are you telling me this, why isn't Marco here now?"

"Marco has always cared deeply about his private life and that now includes you which means you are not allowed to be on his father's radar."

"You act like his dad is dangerous," I said, laughing.

Veronica did not respond right away. She arched an eyebrow and took a slow drink before shrugging her shoulders.

"Is he? Dangerous?" I asked. "It's his dad."

"Luis Amador is his father but he is not Marco's family," Veronica said. "I am his family and now you are too. I told Marco you would become a complication for him but he went ahead anyway, so now I need to help him clean up his mess."

"You think I'm a mess that needs to be cleaned up?" I asked.

"Oh quit being so literal," she said. "You should be flattered that Marco sent me downstairs to stop you. If he didn't give a shit he would have allowed you to come upstairs and prance around in your too tiny skirt and stupid high heel shoes like the other empty headed girls he has paraded around before."

"Not really making me feel better," I said, wishing for more whiskey.

"You dress fine," she said, nodding to my black skirt and tailored white blouse.

"I'm glad you approve."

"But you are much too sensitive," she said, rolling her

eyes.

"Well, let me explain to you what just happened to me," I said, knowing my tone was biting. "I came to see my boyfriend who supposedly loves me, was intercepted by his beautiful *sister*, who explains to me that I can't go upstairs since I may run into my boyfriend's dangerous dad, but don't worry if I was a total slut, he would have paraded me around per normal."

"Yes, exactly," Veronica deadpanned.

"You know this is weird."

"Yes, I do."

"So, I think I'm going to go then," I said, standing this time. "Thanks for the drink. Let my boyfriend know that I'm sorry we couldn't see each other. Maybe we can arrange to meet somewhere even more discrete, a seedy hotel on Aurora perhaps."

My hands shook with anger. I felt as though Marco had disrespected me. Made me feel like an affair, like a lie. I knew I was tapping into my feelings about my father and his adulterous lies but I couldn't stop myself. "Maybe he can buy me a burner phone so there is no record of me calling him."

"He already has a phone for you," Veronica said. "He was supposed to give it to you last week. Would you please sit."

"What?" Heart pounding I stared at her unreadable expression. "You aren't kidding, or wait, you're kidding."

"If you would slow down and stop behaving like a jealous schoolgirl, you might realize that you believe me. You believe all of it, don't you?"

Tears flooded my eyes and I bit my lip to keep from crying. I sank back into the booth. I hated feeling confused and out of control. Did I believe Veronica? Did I believe that Marco loved me and wanted to keep me safe from his family?

"Will I see him tonight?" I said, my mouth dry and body longing for his touch.

"I'm afraid not," she said. "I have been instructed to drive you home or send you home in a cab."

"Get me some black coffee. I can drive in a little while, I've had two drinks," I said.

"Those were double shots," she smiled. "One coffee coming up and I'll follow you home to make sure you get there safely."

"Deal."

Veronica returned with a cup of strong coffee. I sat sipping it in the dark. With every minute that passed I could feel the caffeine settling my mind, diffusing the warm blur of the alcohol. I'd be fine to drive soon.

Veronica and I did not speak. The lounge singer returned from her break. She wore a sparkling sheath dress and closed her eyes while she sang making me feel as though I'd fallen inside some noir film.

But this wasn't a film, this was real life, my life and my real life was officially out of control.

I was Odessa Starr, an independent intelligent woman who was used to being totally self-sufficient and here I was sitting in a bar like an ill-informed damsel in distress.

Was this the price I would pay for Marco's love?

"You ready?" Veronica clapped as the singer completed an almost macabre rendition of "Tiny Dancer." "We have time to make it across the lobby and into the garage." She glanced at her phone. I no longer asked any questions, I assumed she'd gotten a signal from upstairs somehow.

We strode across the lobby to the back staircase. Todd stood by the elevator on guard. He nodded at me as we passed. "Good night miss," he said, a sad smile crossing his face, at least it looked sad to me.

I slipped down the back staircase and tried to tell myself that once I talked to Marco everything would be all right again but I knew it was a lie. Marco loved me and perhaps I loved him too but suddenly everything felt wrong. This felt unfixable to me, it felt broken, well beyond the reach of the love we shared in his four poster bed.

CHAPTER 14

I awoke the next morning; the memory of the night before felt like a weight inside my chest. I was grateful for the routine of the hospital, I didn't even mind hitting traffic on my morning commute. It felt normal and reminded me of my days before Marco when life made more sense to me.

The dark gray skies of the morning felt ominous. I found myself glancing in the rear view mirror afraid of what I might find. I passed a beige Taurus with tinted windows idling in the garage and I wondered who was sitting behind the wheel.

I parked my car in the staff lot and took a deep breath. I felt as though I was losing my mind.

"You all right?" Dr. Mike stood beside my car with a concerned expression on his face.

"Yeah, I'm fine. Didn't sleep well," I said, getting out of the car. For once I was grateful for his company. "Should we walk in together?"

"Sure." He looked a little surprised but pleased. At least that was how I read the expression behind his wire rimmed glasses. "You sure you're okay?" He asked, as we walked through the automatic doors into the orca lobby.

"Sure, I'm great. Just some personal stuff."

"Odessa," Dr. Mike grabbed my hand as I turned to go. "If you need anything. If I can help let me know. We were friends before we were anything else and I miss that. I really do."

"Thanks Mike, I appreciate that," I said, squeezing his hand back. And I meant it. Sleeping with Dr. Mike had been a mistake. But it had been my mistake. It didn't mean he was a bad person, if anything I was the one who led him on. I should have left the moment I knew we were not on the same page instead of waiting six months. "Hey I'm sorry about how things ended between us," I said, shocked that I was bringing up something so personal but it suddenly felt foolish of me to leave things unspoken with the people I cared about.

He smiled. "Thanks Odessa, me too." And we stood like that looking at each other for a moment and I felt something heal between us. As I walked the halls that day I thought about how odd it was that as Marco and I fell apart Dr. Mike and I may have finally found our way back to each other as friends.

* * * *

Why wasn't Marco calling me? All day I jumped at the sound of footsteps or the buzz of my phone. I kept expecting to turn and see him standing there with flowers. I wanted to read a message from him, something apologetic that would make me forget all of my confusion and fear.

But instead there was silence.

I finally broke down and sent a text during lunch time. I sat in the staff room my untouched bento box on the table in front of me. I wasn't hungry, I wasn't thirsty, I felt nervous and utterly dependent, both emotions that threatened my sanity.

We need to talk. Tonight.

I felt sick to my stomach as I waited for him to respond seconds felt like minutes as I stared at that damn phone. I had about given up when my phone buzzed.

Thank God.

Relief washed over me but it was short lived.

Not good tonight. I'll contact you.

Not good? My pulse skyrocketed and my cheeks burned.

Unacceptable. I need answers. Now.

Silence.

Or this relationship is over.

I sent the final text before I had time to reel it back in, to second guess myself, to acknowledge the terror in my heart that Marco and I were headed towards some awful parting.

Odessa I need time.

I fired off a response.

Total truth. You promised me.

I typed those two words and sat completely still. I felt as though I were free falling off a cliff. Marco and I were breaking up. I was going to push him so hard that I'd give him no choice. Veronica had told me to be patient, which was exactly what I wasn't doing.

My phone vibrated with his answer. I closed my eyes afraid to read his response but I needed to know, I had to know. Were we over?

I'll come to you. Tonight. Don't give up on me. Don't give up on us.

Don't give up on me. Don't give up on us.

I stared at his words knowing that if I was looking for my easy out this was it. I didn't need to manufacture a break up, I could simply write back that this was too much, too weird. I could tap out and I'd never have to see Marco Amador again.

My whole body tensed. I needed his touch. I craved his hands on my body; I'd never felt so satisfied and so sure of a lover.

Who was I kidding, I no longer had a choice. My body

and soul had chosen Marco Amador the moment we kissed on New Year's Eve.

I took a deep breath and responded.

Tonight.

And one more thought.

I won't give up.

Holy shit. I really was all in.

* * * *

It was past 10:00 p.m. and I still wore my scrubs when Marco rang the buzzer at my apartment.

"Can I come up?" He asked, his voice tired and worried.

My body ached for him. I wanted to take him in my arms, pull him into my bed and make him forget his worries. I wanted to touch his lips and feel his hands against my skin. I wanted him to make me moan, to erase my fears and go back to the way we were just a few days before.

I said nothing and hit the button, afraid of what my voice would reveal.

I needed to be strong. The man owed me answers and I couldn't allow myself to back down without getting the truth.

I opened the door.

Marco reached for me, his hands around my waist so

quickly my mind didn't have time to tell my body not to respond. He pressed his lips against mine without a single word. There was only his kiss, his tongue pressing into my mouth.

My legs wrapped around his waist, I held on and kissed him back unable to resist. With a single turn he pushed me up against the wall as I buried my face in his neck kissing his skin. He lowered me to the floor, fumbling with the waistband of my scrubs, his hand finding my panties. He parted my lips and slid inside my wet pussy. He moaned as he felt my wetness, his fingers pushing inside me, his lips against mine.

I cried out in pleasure as I tore at the front of his button down shirt exposing his smooth chest.

He slid his fingers out of me and lifted off my shirt exposing the thin white tank I wore over my black bra. Tugging at his belt, I undid his pants pulling them down over his hips exposing his enormous erection.

"Condom," he gasped, gesturing for his pants which were bunched around his ankle.

I reached down and grabbed a package from his back pocket. I felt as though I couldn't unwrap it fast enough.

All my rules, all my boundaries crumbled in the arms of this man. The moment he touched me my body opened up for him with an ache and a need that I found impossible to resist.

"Take me," I whispered, sheathing him quickly. He hooked his arm under one of my legs and lifted me as his cock slid inside me.

I gasped as he pinned me up against the wall.

He grabbed my other leg and I gripped him with my arms raising myself up and down, I rode him, my clit rubbing against him bringing me closer and closer to coming.

His mouth against mine, he kissed me hungrily as he fucked me faster and faster, then harder against the wall.

My thighs clenched and body tensed. He drove into me harder and harder, the pressure so strong I cried out as the orgasm rippled through my body.

Marco kept pounding into me as I came around him, the waves of pleasure continued until I felt him pulse deep inside me. His head dropped onto my shoulder.

"I was so afraid I'd lost you," he whispered, leaning his head against my shoulder. "So afraid."

He lifted me slowly, and my body throbbed as he placed me on my feet.

Then he looked at me, running his fingers along my jawline, his deep brown eyes locked on mine. "I'm so sorry about yesterday," he said. He looked sad, sad and tired.

"I need answers," I said, pulling his face towards mine so our foreheads touched. "If we are going to be together I need to know everything. No secrets. You have no idea how hard this is for me. I wanted to run." I almost cried but managed to take a deep breath and keep the tears at bay.

"I thought I could make it go away," he said, softly. "I wanted to protect you from all this, protect us and I failed."

I felt a coldness in my belly. What could Marco tell me that was so awful? I spent so much time focusing on my own commitment issues it never occurred to me that he may hold a secret so horrible that it would drive us apart.

"You have to tell me," I said. "Secrets will destroy us."

I took his hand and led him across the hardwood to my queen sized bed in the corner of my studio. Covered by a white duvet and enormous pillows. I scooted across the bed and pulled him next to me so we were laying side by side. We were both half-dressed and I was tempted to roll him over on his back and ride him again. I could tell from the way he ran his hands up and down my body that he felt the same way but sex would just delay the inevitable. We needed to talk this out.

"Once I tell you this truth, Odessa. You will be involved," he closed his eyes and exhaled.

"I'm already involved," I said, leaning over and kissing his ear. "Talk."

Marco moved his hand off my body and sighed. He sat up in the bed a little higher. I scooted beside him and leaned my head on his shoulder. The shades open, we could see outside into the night sky. It wasn't the canvas of stars that we shared from his four poster bed at the top of the world, but it was a glimpse of the same universe. I felt as though we belonged in that starlight, we belonged in the cool blue light that bathed our bodies as we intertwined and made love again and again.

"My father is not a good man, Odessa," he said.

I kept my focus on the night sky and ran my fingers gently up and down his chest as he spoke.

"It has taken me a long time to understand the nature of my family's business, of my father's business," he said pausing.

"My mother tried to warn me before she died. She told me that I would need to be strong, to be true to myself. I have failed her so many times."

"You were just a boy when she died," I said. "Weren't you only sixteen? How were you expected . . ."

"I knew then that something was wrong in our household. I sensed it, the tension between my parents. The more successful my father became, the worse things grew between them." he said. "My mother drowned on a family boating trip in Cabo San Lucas. She fell off the boat while we were anchored near the harbor. It was the middle of the night, I didn't even know she was missing until the next day."

"You were so young," I whispered, my heart aching for his grief as a boy and as a grown man.

"I learned last year that in the days before my mother's accident she planned to leave my father. She planned to take me away and start a new life but she never got the chance."

"How did you find out?"

"Veronica," he said. "Her mother had secured us new passports and an apartment in Brooklyn. We never made it."

I had so many questions but I stayed silent. My hand running up and down Marco's chest tracing the lines of the tattoo on his arm as I let him speak; I let him share his truth with me.

"My mother wanted to leave my father because she discovered that our family fortune was tied to the Mexican drug cartel."

My hand froze.

"My father's import and export business is profitable but he distributes more than just high end furniture around the globe. He distributes product for the Mexican mafia."

"Your mother found out." I was frozen, unable to move.

"My father told me the truth about the business last year, I think he thought I would be pleased to be a part of the family empire, grateful even. I always suspected that the numbers didn't add up. Amador Shipping has been wildly successful but we were making too much money for the industry. A recession hit the country but it did not impact our books. We continued to make money. For years I knew something was wrong, but I was afraid to dig deeper. I was afraid to pull back the curtain and face the monster that is my father. But I'm not afraid anymore," he said. "I am done behaving like a frightened child.

"I will do whatever it takes to destroy his business. My mother wanted no part of it and it's taken me years to see the path. The trouble is that there is so much corruption in Mexico, any time the government gets close to connecting my father with the Cartel someone dies or stops talking. Amador Shipping has numerous legitimate sources of income that makes it hard to know which contract is real and which is a shell contract for drug transport.

"Once I knew the truth about the business, Veronica told me about my mother's failed plan to escape."

"You think your father killed her," I said, slowly unsure whether it was right to verbalize something so painful, so wrong.

Marco nodded. "Things are moving quickly now. Luis's visit last night was unscheduled, which means either he really wanted to speak to me or he was hoping to catch me off guard."

"Do you think he knows you are working with the DEA?"

"He may be an evil son of a bitch, but he isn't stupid," Marco said. "I need to disappear."

"Disappear." My heart raced, hot tears filled my throat.

"Not for forever, just until the case gets wrapped up. I need to disappear and I want you to come with me."

"You want me to give up my life . . ." I said, feeling sick to my stomach. I couldn't lose Marco, I couldn't bear it, but what choice did I have?

"I have money hidden away from my father. Legitimate holdings that I've managed to separate and hide in off-shore accounts. If I leave, when I leave, there will be more than enough money to live a very comfortable life and my hope is it won't be forever."

"How long?" My vision blurred with tears.

"I don't know, a year maybe longer."

"The study at the hospital, I'd have to leave it," I whispered. My chest felt hot, breathing constricted.

"I am a selfish bastard for even asking you," he said. "But I can't bear the idea of a life without you in it. Will you disappear with me?"

"When? How much time do I have to decide?" I wanted to sob, I wanted to scream and yell at Marco and at his father. I'd promised myself I would never give up my identity for any man, and now Marco wanted me to walk away from my life completely, no questions asked.

"We don't have much time," he said, rolling over towards me. "We have two days."

"Forty-eight hours?" I felt nauseous.

"Veronica will have the details, but the idea is I disappear and the next time I see Luis is in a courtroom."

"But then it's over. You give your father up to the Feds and then you can let everything go, right?"

"Perhaps," he said, running his finger along the ridge of my collar bone. He slipped his hand under the fabric of my tank top finding my breasts. "There is a risk that even if I succeed in stopping my father the number of people he's connected to would make being me difficult but not impossible. Nothing would be the same for us ever again."

I swallowed. "Is it worth it?"

"It's worth it," he said, kissing my neck. "It's worth it to do the right thing. To be true to who I am. To avenge my mother and save people from the evil my father spreads in this world." He moved down my body raising my tank top up he slipped it over my head. I lay on the bed, naked from the waist down, in my black bra. He reached behind my back and unclipped the bra.

"It's worth it to make love to a woman like you, to tell you my truth and know that even if I lose you, you'll know that I loved you. I love you with everything I am." He lay on top of me, supporting his weight on his elbows, I felt him grow hard.

"I love you Odessa Starr," he said, his voice husky. "I will love you and only you for the rest of my life."

"You don't know that," I whispered. "If you leave without me, you don't know what will happen."

"Yes, I do." He smiled, his mouth on my neck and moving down my body. He kissed the top of my breast, his breath changing with need. "From the moment I touched you, it's you, it's only been you."

He took my nipple in his mouth and sucked biting down as he slid his hand between my legs and circled the hardening nub of my clitoris.

I moaned and spread my legs pulling him towards me. I had condoms in my night stand and reached for one, unwrapping it and sliding it on him.

"I love you," he said, pushing inside me.

I arched my back and moaned.

"I love you," he said again, pushing deeper and pushing my legs back. I arched my back pushing up against him.

"Tell me again," I said. "Again and again."

His cock inside me he rocked in and out each time making me moan louder and louder. His thrusting grew deeper and harder but always stimulating my clit. I felt myself building towards a climax, a connection binding us together until I came, pleasure rippling through my body.

Marco whispered in my ear, "I love you Odessa Starr, I will love you forever."

I turned and whispered back. "I love you too, I love you Marco. I love you . . ." And he kissed until we fell asleep intertwined in each other's bodies.

* * * *

We made love two more times that night. Each time was frantic and hungry. I felt as though we were making love in case the world ended.

We made love as if we would never see each other again.

When I woke in the morning Marco was dressing. He kissed my forehead.

"I'll see you tonight," he said. "You think about what you want. I love you no matter what you choose."

I watched him leave my apartment, light filtering into the room, it looked so familiar but felt all new to me. Making love to Marco inside these four walls had changed things for me. This bedroom belonged to us now. I just wasn't sure if there would be an us in forty-eight hours. I loved Marco, this much was true, but did I love him enough to walk away from my life forever?

CHAPTER 15

I had forty-eight hours to walk away from my life or lose the man I loved.

After Marco left, I lay in bed and stared at the cream colored ceiling of my apartment. For the first time, I noticed tiny cracks in the plaster that looked vaguely like the Eiffel Tower if I squinted at them long enough. I thought of Paris, the city of lovers. There were so many places I wanted to go with Marco. Depending on how I looked at it, traveling the world with Marco was one decision away.

If we ran away together, we would have freedom and he claimed that money would never be an issue. We could spend weeks on remote beaches tangled together. We could stay up too late and sleep in even later. But what if we got bored of each other? What if this fiery love burned too hot and too fast and we were left staring at each other with nothing to say?

My heart pounded against the walls of my chest. I closed my eyes as I inhaled acutely aware of every muscle in my body, nerves thrumming with energy.

All of my worries about where we would go and how

long we would last were just white noise distracting me from my real decision.

I needed to decide if I was willing to walk away from the life I had built for myself to be with the man I loved.

"Get out of bed, Odessa," I whispered to myself throwing my feet onto the cold hardwood floor and willing myself across the room for a shower.

It was time to go to work.

If I decided to stay, I needed to keep doing my job.

And if I decided to go? With the shower running, I stood in front of the bathroom mirror as steam filled the tiny room erasing my reflection.

If I decided to go, I needed to wrap up my life in forty-eight hours. No matter what I chose, it was time to get to work.

* * * *

I needed to talk to someone. Shea had already left for the day, so I made plans to meet her for lunch near the hospital.

"Tell me what is going on," Shea said, sliding into the booth across from me at Valermo's Pizza. "Your message totally freaked me out and you don't eat at places like this. Something is wrong."

The waitress, a skinny college aged girl, approached

our table with a pitcher of ice water. Shea's green eyes locked on me, eyebrows raised as she waited for the girl to fill our glasses.

"I have a problem," I said, keeping my voice low. "A problem that I can't really share with anyone, but I need to talk to someone."

"Talk to me," Shea said, immediately reaching across the table and grasping my hand.

"I am so sorry about all of this . . ." I said, my eyes growing wet with tears. This was going to be harder than I thought.

"Honey, what is wrong?" Shea asked dropping her voice to a whisper. "Are you dying?"

"No, God no," I sniffed, a few tears spilling over and running down my cheeks.

The waitress returned to our table, her wide smile dropping at the sight of my expression. "So . . . are you ready to order? I can tell you about the special it's . . ."

Shea interrupted. "We'll take a medium deep dish combo pizza with extra cheese, extra pepperoni, and two Pyramid Ales."

"All righty," the girl said, taking notes.

"Shea, I can't drink and go back to work." I wiped my nose with a napkin.

"You can have a beer," she said. "God knows I could use one and I am not drinking alone."

The waitress looked at me, hand poised above her little notebook. "You in for a beer?"

"I'm in, sure, I'll drink one, thanks."

"Pizza and beer it is," the girl's smile returned and she bounced away back to the kitchen. She seemed so carefree, so young with nothing but possibility in front of her. I felt there was possibility for me, I just wasn't sure how to live with either of my choices.

"You are killing me here," Shea said leaning forward. "So, you aren't dying which is awesome by the way. What else . . . Are you pregnant?"

"No," I said.

"Are you getting sued?"

"No."

"Did you kill someone? Get caught shoplifting? Decide to go gluten free?"

"No, no, and no," I said, actually laughing a little.

Shea sighed. "So, you can either tell me or I'll keep firing questions at you, we can do this the hard way or the easy way little lady. My daddy always said it is best to just get the hard stuff off your chest . . ."

I leaned forward. "Marco's family is a part of the

Mexican drug cartel," I whispered, leaning forward.

Shea's jaw dropped.

"It's not Marco, it's his father, Luis. Apparently he is the brains behind the organization."

"So, that's where all their money comes from?" Shea said, rocking back in her seat. She looked shell shocked.

The waitress delivered two beers. Shea picked one up and took a few large gulps.

"There is a lot I don't know, but apparently Amador Shipping was a legitimate business once upon a time, but that changed."

"No shit."

"No, shit," I said, taking a sip of my beer. The glass was wet and cold. "You know I don't even like beer."

"I know," Shea said. "But since they don't serve the hard stuff here . . . so, drugs. That's bad, like really bad. So, is Marco a dealer?"

"No, he isn't, he wants out." I rubbed my temples. "Marco has been working with the feds against his father."

Shea stared at me and chugged the rest of her beer. "So, what are you going to do? Are you going to break up with him?"

"Marco's asked me to go away with him."

"Go away, like on vacation, or move?"

"As in disappear," I whispered. Our waitress returned with our medium sized pizza pie, grease pooled on top of the meat.

Without taking her eyes off of me, Shea blotted two slices with a napkin and made plates for us both. "This is sounding very scary. Very scary and very dangerous. I don't like it."

"It is, scary," I said. "There is some chance that if Marco testifies against his father that some of his father's business partners would retaliate."

"You can't be a part of this," Shea whispered. "This is too dangerous."

"I love him Shea," I said, my voice high and thin. "I love him so much it scares me. He's like oxygen in my world. I am not sure how I can live without him, but I'm not sure how I can leave either." I bit my lip and looked skyward waving my hands in front of my eyes trying to keep the tears under control.

The gravity of my choice felt so heavy to me right then. It was as if I'd swallowed a cold, hard stone. I was sick with the weight of it pressing against my heart and lungs.

Shea's eyes bugged and she leaned forward and grasped my hand again with greasy fingers. "This is wonderful!" She practically squealed. "I mean it's fucking terrible, but it's so wonderful. You are in love Odessa. You are crazy in love with Marco."

"No, it's not wonderful," I said, still fanning my eyes. "I'm in love with a man who has connections to a violent and terrifying criminal element."

"But he's doing what's right, he's taking a stand," Shea said, sounding almost wistful.

"He is trying," I said, smiling. "I think it takes a lot of courage to face your family. I think I love him more now that I understand what he is facing. I hate the situation but I love him even more."

"Do you trust him?" Shea said, staring into my eyes.

"Yes," I said, without hesitation. A few weeks ago I would have found it impossible to trust any man. I hadn't trusted a man with my heart since my dad betrayed our family. Marco Amador seduced me and showed me how to be vulnerable with my body and my heart.

"Is he in love with you?" Shea said. "Who am I kidding of course he is." She laughed.

I managed a half smile through my tears. "Yes, he loves me. He loves me with all his heart and I believe him. Can you believe this is me talking?"

"No, I mean yes," Shea said. "I always knew that you would meet a man strong enough to break down those walls someday."

"Figures the guy who does it would ask me to walk away from my life, right?"

"Love is complicated sometimes," Shea said.

I closed my eyes and leaned back against the cracked green vinyl of the booth. Our greasy pizza sat untouched in front of us but we'd both managed to drain our beers. On the wall above us an aged poster for Husky Football proclaiming the old coach the "Dawgfather." I tried to focus on the joke and ignore the mafia undertones of the photo.

"How can I help you my friend," Shea said, her voice warm and her smile trying to reach me.

"I don't know. I just needed to talk."

"You want my opinion?"

"Yes?" I said, weakly. "I just want someone to tell me what to do. Can you believe that? I'm so used to having a plan, to calling the shots and right now I just want someone to decide for me."

"Well, I won't decide for you. Only you can do that," Shea said. "But I can tell you that a life without love is nothing."

"But my job, my research."

"If you choose a life with Marco Amador, you will

find your way together. I have no doubt that you will find a way to channel that brilliant mind of yours and continue your career."

"The study is going well," I sniffed. "Dr. Mike is actually doing a wonderful job leading. It wouldn't be impossible for me to step away. I could leave and the research could continue."

Shea nodded. "If you choose to leave I would miss you terribly and if you choose to stay I will support you until your heart stops hurting."

"Which would be forever."

"Maybe." Shea smiled at me. "I do have one question. It's pretty serious."

"Yeah," I said, blowing my nose in one of those scratchy napkins. I supposed if I was used to crying more in public I would have one of those handy tissue packs, no such luck.

"If you go, can I have your parking place?" Shea wrinkled her nose.

I laughed and threw the napkin towards her.

"That's disgusting," she said, batting the make shift tissue across the table. "Does Marco know the kind of manners you have?"

I looked at my smiling friend and my heart ballooned

with warmth for her and the years we had spent together walking the halls of The Holiday apartment building. Shea loved me enough to tell me to leave, she was such a generous and giving soul. I felt a little bad about not telling her everything. I'd kept out the part about Marco's suspicions that his mother had been killed. I also neglected to tell her I had a short amount of time to choose.

I glanced at the Husky clock at the back of the restaurant. It was already 1:00 p.m. I was about twelve hours into my forty-eight hour countdown. I felt as though my life had been poured into an hourglass, time was running out.

I needed to make a decision and I wanted to make it out of love, not fear, fear of losing, fear of being hurt. I wanted to choose out of love for myself and Marco.

I sensed that whatever I chose would shape the rest of my life.

I have been wrong about a lot of things in my life but I was right about that. Marco had already changed my life; I had just been too slow to know it.

CHAPTER 16

I made it through the rest of the day on auto pilot. Marco had told me he would be in touch and not to worry; I believed him. Whenever I caught a glimpse of a clock, or a watch or heard an alarm that horrible sense of time would overwhelm me. Time, we had so very little of it.

The buzzer in my apartment rang at 9:00 p.m. I jumped to my feet to answer it and pressed the button on the call box. "Marco?" I glanced at my phone. I hadn't missed a call or a text.

"Mr. Amador has sent a car for you miss," a man's voice said.

"Right, thanks," I said. "Be right down." I wasn't totally surprised that Marco had sent a driver. I supposed it was safer than having me drive myself across town. If he wanted to keep me secret, it probably wasn't the best idea to park my car overnight in his private parking space.

I felt a rush of energy as I grabbed my sweater and locked up my apartment. As I walked down the hall I tried to ignore the ticking clock in my mind.

Every hour mattered.

I now had twenty-four hours remaining to make a

choice.

Outside the building a long black limo sat parked in the rain. I dashed outside, rain pelting my face. A tall thing man wearing a black suit opened the back door for me shielding me with a black umbrella.

"Ms. Starr," he said, nodding as I slipped into the darkened back seat. Inside there was a bottle of water in a beverage holder and classical music played. I closed my eyes and relaxed as the car headed downtown the repetitive swoosh of the windshield wipers sounding like a meditation.

The driver pulled into the hotel's underground parking lot near the back staircase where Todd usually met me to help with my bags.

"Where's Todd?" I asked, as the man opened the back door.

"Who?" he said.

"Todd, he works for Mr. Amador," I said.

"Good night miss," the driver said, nodding at me and ignoring my question he left me alone by the back stairs.

* * * *

The elevator doors to the condo opened to silence.

"Marco?" I called, stepping into the stone entry way. A feeling of dread formed in my belly. Where was Todd?

Why hadn't Marco met me at the door? "Hello?" I said, walking across the living room toward the bedroom.

I looked inside, the room was empty. I glanced at my phone and sent a text. "Car arrived," I wrote. "I'm here. Where are you?"

I turned to leave the bedroom when I heard a clicking noise and turned to see Marco behind me.

"Thank God," he said, wrapping his arms around me. His phone beeped in his pocket.

"I just texted you," I said. "Where were you? I was freaking out a bit."

"Sorry, I'm sorry," he said, taking my hand and leading me beside the bed. There was a small door in the wall that I had never noticed before mainly because it had no doorknob that I could see and was painted to match the walls.

"Is that a panic room?" I asked, pointing to the darkened space.

"Yes," he said. "I'm sorry, I don't mean to scare you. I've never used the damn thing before, but Veronica wanted me to access it, make sure I could get inside if necessary."

"This is getting really scary isn't it," I said, leaning into him.

"It is," he kissed my forehead. "But we have tonight and if we need to, we can jump inside this soundproof fallout shelter until the troops arrive to save us."

"You are serious about protecting me, aren't you," I whispered looking up into his dark brown eyes.

"If the zombie apocalypse starts, I mean *when* the zombie apocalypse starts, you and I will have a place to hide out. We can live like royalty in a ten by ten foot space."

"Can I see it?" I asked, smiling and taking his hand. We had so much to discuss, I had a decision to make, but there was only one thing I wanted to do with the hours I had left and it didn't include keeping my clothes on. "You did say it was sound proof?" I grinned.

Marco looked at me, a crooked half smile crossing his face. He wore his trademark black cashmere turtle neck, and slim fitted jeans. "I suppose we could find out," he said, taking both my hands in his and backing through the panic room door.

He hit a key pad on the wall and the door closed behind us with a whooshing sound. We stood in a small square room with concrete floors, a cot, and racks of storage along one wall.

"How long do you think we would survive in here," I whispered my hands sliding up under his shirt, my fingertips tingled as I brushed against his bare skin.

"Forever, as long as we are together." He dropped his forehead against mine and backed me up slowly towards the cot. The room was dark with a soft yellow light overhead and a faint blue glow from the keypad.

"I want you," I whispered, pulling him towards me. I could feel the hardness of him pushing against me as I brushed my hand against his pants.

He answered me with a kiss, his mouth against mine with a hunger that made me moan. I fumbled with his belt as he pushed my skirt up and pushed me down on the cot.

I unsheathed him from his pants and brushed against his throbbing hardness with my fingertips. I loved feeling him bare against me.

I scooted back on the bed as he climbed over me. My panties still on, he ran his hand along the inside of my thigh plunging his fingers inside my wetness. I clenched my thighs together locking him inside.

"Protection," I gasped, fumbling for my purse which I'd dropped to the ground. I pulled out a condom and unrolled it my mouth never leaving his lips, my pussy clenched tightly around his fingers. He sheathed himself and parted my legs teasing me with his enormous cock through the thin silk of my underwear.

"Now, please," I gasped, reaching for my underwear. He gripped my hand and instead grasped the fabric of my panties.

"You need to be fucked Ms. Starr," he whispered, his eyes locking with mine.

"Yes, Mr. Amador," I said.

He smiled and with one hand tore my panties off and then plunged deep inside me. I screamed with pleasure and rocked backward wanting to ride his hardness.

My back was against the soft blanket on the cot. I wrapped my legs around him as he pushed into me again and again. I tilted myself up as high as I could while still riding him up and down, driving him between my legs. He was in control but I could feel how he let me direct our energy at times.

The climax came hard and fast. My body released and I felt nothing but him inside of me, nothing but the sensation of our bodies connecting as one and the raw need that we felt for each other.

I needed this. I wanted this. I wanted to be fucked by this man forever no matter what the cost.

Marco pushed deep inside me with a moan, shaking and shuddering. He collapsed beside me and rolled over kissing my cheek and reaching for his clothes.

I stood and picked up my torn panties twirling them in the air. "You owe me a new pair, you know. First a blouse and now . . ."

Marco looked at me his face ashen, eyes wide. "What car?" he asked.

"What do you mean what car?"

He held his phone in his hand. "You said, I sent a car. I didn't send a fucking car Odessa. How did you get here?"

I felt a rush of fear and anxiety. "A driver came, I thought it was you."

"What did he say?"

"He said . . ." My mind was spinning. "I don't know he said Marco sent a car, no, he said Mr. Amador." I stopped and closed my eyes feeling stupid. "He said Mr. Amador sent a car. It wasn't you, was it. It was your father."

Marco strode to the key pad and punched in some numbers. "He knows who you are," he said. "This changes everything."

"What does it change?" I gasped, panic racing through my veins. I followed him across the room as he dialed his phone.

"Veronica," he said, his voice dropping as he turned away from me. "Luis has identified Odessa. Is there security downstairs?"

I stopped in the center of the living room feeling sick; this was my fault, I had been so stupid. I should have checked with him about the car. I should have been smarter, more careful. I sank into the couch that faced the silver tree and the bird cages that Marco had given me just a month before. New Year's Eve felt like years ago. I felt as though Marco and I had spent years together, and now I feared I had made a stupid mistake that would somehow cost me everything.

"I can still disappear with you," I whispered, reaching my hand up as Marco walked past.

He nodded and squeezed my fingers. "Make it happen Veronica," he said. "This needs to happen tomorrow night."

He hung up the phone and turned to me. "Veronica's people are in the lobby. No one is making it upstairs tonight but Luis was sending me a message. He wants me to know that he has discovered you. You need to choose Odessa."

I stood up slowly from the couch, my legs felt weak like I might fall at any moment, but I reached out and held Marco's hand. "I choose you," I whispered feeling a rush of relief flood my body.

"I don't want you choosing out of fear. If you don't go, Veronica can protect you. It's me he's after. Once I'm gone, he will lose interest in you."

"I'm not choosing out of fear," I said, squeezing his hand. "I'm choosing out of love." And as I spoke I knew this was my truth. I wanted to disappear in this man's love, dissolve in the heat of our passion for each other, the warmth of his kisses, the sensation of our bodies joining as one. I wanted to make love to this man every day for the rest of my life. "I believe in you," I said, blood rushing through my head making me almost dizzy. "I believe in us and I don't want to live in a world where we aren't in it together."

Marco wrapped his arms around me in a fierce hug and we stood together unmoving. I had just agreed to walk away from my life for the man I loved. I had never been so happy and so scared all at once.

CHAPTER 17

I awoke in Marco's arms the next morning hazy sunlight filling the bedroom. My heart raced for a moment as I remembered the events of the night before, Marco's proposal that we leave together, my agreement to go with him. I took a breath to calm my heart. I felt safe beside him. I felt safe if we were together.

Marco rolled over and trailed a fingertip across my naked body.

"I want to memorize your skin," he said, kissing my shoulder. "I want every part of you blazed in my mind."

"You don't need to memorize me," I said, turning and taking his face in my hand, trying to look more happy than afraid. "We're in this together now. Remember?"

"I remember," he said, his voice heavy with emotion.

"What time do we leave?" I asked. "And how are we leaving exactly?"

"Right." Marco cleared his throat, rolled over and checked his phone. "Veronica said she would have instructions this morning. I believe the pickup time is 7:00 p.m."

"And what happens at 7:00 p.m."

"The less we know . . ."

"I mean are we getting on a plane? A boat? A submarine?" My heart hammered in my chest. Staying calm would be more difficult than I thought. "Do I just wait with my bags packed?"

"Veronica is arranging everything. Todd will take you back to your apartment to get your things. You will have time to pack and rest, he'll wait for you. Do not get into a car with anyone unless I tell you." He actually smiled a bit when he said that.

"Can I go to work today?" I asked, staring out the floor to ceiling window of his bedroom. The sky was growing dark with storm clouds approaching across Puget Sound. "If I'm going away, there are things I should do, loose ends . . ."

"I'm sorry, Veronica wants you to call in sick. She says it's too dangerous for you to go to the hospital. I don't think Luis will come after you at work, but we don't know."

"I just wanted one more day there," I said, hot tears flooding my eyes. "I wanted to say good-bye to some of the patients, make sure things will keep running smoothly."

"I'm so sorry," Marco said, his eyes clouding. "Are you sure you can do this? Are you sure you can leave?"

"Yes, I am sure," I said, taking a deep breath and

holding my tears at bay. “If I had a week it wouldn’t be enough time. It’s better to just rip the bandage off now. I’ll get packed and we will leave. Today it happens.” I said, trying not to sound like I was giving myself a pep talk.

I moved to get out of the bed and he grabbed my hand pulling me back under the covers. “Don’t leave, not yet,” he whispered burying his face in my neck. “Let me love you one more time. I need you Odessa, I need to feel you one more time.”

I did not resist, I couldn’t. My hand found his hardness and I stroked him with my fingertips. Then I straddled him, feeling his cock beneath my spread legs. I reached for a condom.

“All I need is this,” I said raising my body up and sliding him inside me. I moaned as he entered me.

“Just this,” Marco whispered grasping my hips with his hands. Together we rode each other, his hands raising me up, my hands on his chest I pushed myself up and down, faster and faster until I could feel the orgasm building. As the ripples came my mouth found his, my pussy shaking and quivering with heat as wave after wave shook me to my bones.

Marco followed right after his back arching as he drove into me deeply his body throbbing and pulsing. We collapsed on top of each other, dripping with sweat, and aching with pleasure.

"You have all of me," I said, giving him one last kiss. "See you tonight."

"Tonight," he said, squeezing my hand.

And with that I walked out of Marco's bedroom and left his four poster bed.

* * * *

Todd drove me to my apartment. I tried not to worry about what exactly that meant as I padded up the stairs to my apartment. I unlocked the door aware that this was the last morning I would open my apartment door.

I made myself a cup of coffee. Again the last time I'd brew coffee in my own place.

I sat down on my bed and took a deep breath. I was about to be late for the Wednesday staff meeting. It was time to call in sick. I fired off an email but with days of absence I needed to leave a message with the staffing nurse.

"Staffing," Dr. Mike surprised me by answering the phone.

"Hey," I said, walking to my window. "It's Odessa. I'm out sick today. Some sort of flu." I braced myself for some biting remark but instead heard nothing but kindness from my ex.

"I'm sorry to hear you are sick, you need anything? Chicken soup? Fluids?"

"No, I need sleep. I definitely need more of that." I wasn't totally lying. I was sleep deprived just not from the flu.

"Okay, well I'll let Marcia know you are out. I was hoping to talk with you before the staff meeting, I've been working on the latest round of results and we are making a difference Odessa. These kids are responding. I think it might be time to appeal for a broader group of patients."

My heart surged at the news. "We could talk on Monday about that," I blurted before realizing there would be no Monday for me. "Put time on my calendar," I added softly. "We can collaborate on a proposal though you don't really need me to move forward here. I'd trust you with the whole program Mike. It's good to know I can take a sick day and you'll be there keeping the ship righted."

As I talked I was grateful for Mike and for all of the traits that had drawn me to him at the start. He was thorough, he cared and he was a brilliant doctor. I needed him to know that I believed in him before I left, I had to know that things would continue without me, or I wouldn't be able to bear it.

"That means a lot coming from you," Dr. Mike said,

his voice soft.

I inhaled to keep the tears from coming. "I'm sorry how things ended between us Mike. I really am. I'm going to make you late to the staff meeting," I added.

"It's all right," he said. "You know when we started dating you told me you didn't want anything serious."

"I did."

"And I tried to change your mind."

"You did," I said, able to smile at the memory of his attempts to get me to move in with him out of logic. There was the cost savings, the shorter commute, and global warming; he had truly worked all angles.

"I understand now that you weren't ready to be serious with me, and that is okay."

"Mike, it wasn't you."

"No, hear me out," he said. "You will find that person you want to commit to Odessa, it will happen and it will be okay. I wanted to believe that you were just anti-relationship."

"Well, I was . . ."

"No, you were anti-relationship with me," I could hear the smile in his voice. "I can see how happy you are with Marco. I'm glad you two are together. I wanted you to know that."

"Thanks Mike," I said.

"Means a lot coming from the guy who has spent the last month making snide comments?"

"Yeah," I laughed. "It does."

"Feel better Odessa," he said. "I'll start drafting the study expansion proposal today, we can review it next week."

"Sounds great," I said, tears choking my voice. "Thanks Mike, bye." I hung up the phone before sobs wracked through my body.

I needed to be strong. I needed to be okay with saying good-bye.

CHAPTER 18

Marco finally sent a text.

Go outside. Todd will drive you.

I responded quickly, my heart racing.

I love you. Be there soon.

I stood in the center of my apartment. I'd tidied up the kitchen and left my good wine out on the counter. The refrigerator was empty; I'd wanted to make sure nothing rotted. I wasn't about to leave Billie with a mess to clean up or worse Shea.

I felt terribly sad knowing I couldn't say good-bye to Shea, Billie, Bella, or anyone at the hospital. I thought of my mother and wondered what I would say to her if I called; I couldn't say good-bye, she was fragile at best. I'd find a way to reach out to her, to tell her I was safe.

I took a mental picture of the apartment, the view into the alley, the uneven stucco walls and cracked ceiling, the pale hardwood floors, and the green and white molding. I'd spent more than four years in this tiny studio. The bare walls had never bothered me and now they looked empty and sad. My bed . . . I had slept a full night in my bed only once in the past month. I didn't live here anymore. This place was no longer my home. Home was with Marco.

"Good-bye," I said, tears blurring my vision. I clicked off the light and locked my door.

As I walked down the hall, I noticed that the large two bedroom apartment next door was vacant. The door wide open the smell of fresh cleanser drifted into the hall.

New neighbors I thought. Neighbors I'd never meet.

Holding my single bag of belongings I walked down the stairs never once looking back.

* * * *

Todd took my bag and held open the car door.

"Where are we going?" I asked, sliding into the smooth black leather in the backseat of the Tesla.

"I'm not supposed to tell you," Todd said, cringing. "I'm sorry, but we'll be there soon," he offered.

"All right," I said, taking a deep breath. "Now get me out of here before I change my mind."

He closed the door and we pulled away from the curb.

Our destination was Elliot Bay Marina. I was shocked to realize my next great adventure with Marco was destined to start at such a normal location. The parking lot was packed with cars and people coming and going on their way to one of the restaurants along the waterfront. Todd parked and opened the door for me my bag in hand.

It wasn't terribly late but the sun set early in the winter time.

"This way miss," Todd said, softly. I wrapped my arms around myself my breath freezing in bursts as I followed Todd across the lot.

He turned and smiled and I thought of how much he had changed since the first night he'd checked the little black book that granted me access upstairs. Todd had looked so freckle faced and young. Now he had bags under his eyes and his jaw was tense. These days were hard on everyone close to Marco, not just me.

We passed a darkened shop window with a blue and yellow neon sign in the shape of a NYC skyline hanging overhead. Manhattan Galleries the sign buzzed and flickered in the evening light. Marco had always said he would take me to Theo's gallery. I felt as though Marco and I were coming full circle. We had met at a table filled with Theo Manhattan's art and here I was disappearing with Marco steps from the gallery.

Todd stopped walking when we reached the end of the parking lot. He pointed down a gradual bank with a paved path that led to beach access of the Sound. It was a cold and miserable night with a biting wind. White caps crashed onto the shoreline below.

On a level stretch of rock up from the beach, Marco and Veronica argued. The wind was too strong for me to make out their words. They stood beside a shiny black helicopter with an enormous gold A on its side on what looked like a private helicopter pad.

I stopped in my tracks. Why were we taking a helicopter from the Amador fleet? And why were they fighting? This didn't feel right to me but I wasn't sure how I was supposed to feel on a night like this anyway.

Marco looked up at me and held up a hand indicating I should stay where I was. He turned and seemed to shout something more at Veronica. She stood, arms crossed her face unreadable and walked to the helicopter as Marco walked up the hillside towards me.

My heart fluttered as I watched him jump off the rocky terrain onto the paved switchback trail that tourists used to walk to the shoreline. He wore a black coat and a cap over his head. Over my shoulder were the window seats of Palisades with views of the water. If we took off from here we would be clearly visible to scores of diners.

My heart pounded and I gripped my single leather bag in my hand, palms sweating as Marco approached.

Then everything happened very quickly.

The helicopter propeller sprang to life with a roar,

kicking up more wind.

"Marco!" I shouted as he reached me.

"Odessa!"

With his arms around me, I buried my face in his chest and looked up into his eyes. We stood beneath a street lamp, bathed in yellow light. "Where are we going?" I shouted

Marco didn't answer right away, the helicopter's spotlight turned on passing over us with a blinding white light.

I blinked my eyes seeing spots.

"Change of plans!" Marco shouted, his arms on my shoulder. I thought I'd misheard him.

"What?"

"Change of plans! You aren't coming with me," he shouted even louder.

"No, no you can't do this. No!"

He held me at arm's length as I struggled against his grip, dropping my bag, throwing punches at the air.

"You need to trust me Odessa!" He shouted.

"No, we are going together!" I gasped, still struggling.

"This is the only way. You can't give up your life. I won't do that to you."

"It's too late! It's done!" I cried, tears pouring down my face. Marco turned away from me, still holding me in place. I struggled to get in front of him, to look him in the eyes. "Don't do this, Why are you doing this?" I sobbed.

He pulled me close, his voice next to my ear. "You need to trust me. Trust us. Everything will be okay. I love you." Then he kissed me, his lips hard and fierce against mine and I felt him turn to go as another set of hands gripped me around the waist.

Veronica.

"No!" I screamed kicking and struggling against her.

"Come with me!" She shouted pulling me away from my viewpoint.

"No! No! No!"

Behind us in the parking lot a small crowd had gathered under a covered stretch of walkway with a clear view of my breakdown and the spinning helicopter.

"What is going on?" I gasped, sobbing and finally stopping. "I don't understand what is happening. Why is he leaving without me?"

Veronica said nothing but loosened her grip enough so I could turn and see the helicopter rise into the air. It buzzed the marina twice giving everyone a clear view before pivoting and heading out to sea.

Light glinted off the enormous gold A on the helicopter's side. I stood in shock watching the love of my life disappear into the blackness riding in one of his father's fleet.

"You lied to me," I said to Veronica. The deafening sound of the helicopter dropped to a soft hum as it moved farther away.

"You need to go home," Veronica said, her expression revealing nothing. "Todd will drive you."

"I'm not going anywhere with you people!" I shouted.

There was a tremendous flash of light followed by a deafening boom. People screamed behind me.

I turned to see the helicopter spiraling and ablaze.

"Marco! Marco! No!" I pushed past Veronica screaming.

The helicopter zig zagged across the sky before hitting the water. It hovered above the waves glowing orange and red then sank beneath the surface.

"Marco!" I sobbed, falling to my knees and sinking into the dirt and mud beside the trail. "Call 911!" I shouted at Veronica. "Call the police! Do something! Do anything!"

Veronica offered me her hand, her face a mask. "Let me help you," she said. "There is nothing we can do here."

"No!" I swatted at her hand and stood on my own. The crowd under the walkway had grown larger. People held up cell phones taking videos and making calls. I heard the distant sound of sirens.

"Don't be stupid Odessa," Veronica said. "Todd will take you home. Marco wouldn't want you out here like this."

"Don't talk to me about what he wanted," I spat at her, unsteady and sobbing. "He wanted me to go, didn't he; he wanted me to go and you stopped him. That's what you were fighting about."

"I'm not going to answer that," she said her voice cold.

Todd approached his eyes wide and glistening with tears. "Please Miss," he said, reaching for me. "Let me take you home."

"No, not you, I'm not going with any of you," I stumbled past them moving toward the crowd. Marco was dead. I felt as though my heart had been torn from my chest. I couldn't breathe. I needed to breathe. Lights blurred and I heard voices but I couldn't make sense of anything as I fought my way through the crowd.

"Amador helicopter . . ."

I needed to get away.

"I think that was the son."

I had to escape.

"Doubt there were survivors."

I had to keep moving.

I felt a strong hand on my arm and looked into a

familiar set of pale blue eyes. In my panic I couldn't remember his name but I knew his face, I knew that Marco trusted him.

"Help me!" I whispered, grabbing his arm. "Help me, don't let them take me."

"Easy, easy," he said, moving me out of the rain and under cover.

Veronica and Todd appeared beside him. "Thank God," Veronica said, "We'll take care of her," she said. reaching for me. I backed away and pushed against the man's chest.

"She's in shock," the man said.

"We'll take care of her, I'm a friend." Veronica stepped forward. "She's upset."

"She's not a friend," I whispered. "She is a liar, a liar . . ."

"Right. Well, I don't believe she wants to go with you," the man said. "It's a bit of a problem you see."

Veronica stepped toward him. "You don't know what you are doing."

"That may be true, but I know this woman is hysterical and she doesn't want you to touch her." The man stood his ground stepping protectively in front of me.

Veronica looked from me to him, as if she were weighing her options. "Make sure she gets home."

Todd nodded and handed my bag to the man and they walked away.

"You want to sit for a minute?" The man asked. His face kind, and he had an accent, British I believed.

"Yes, yes please," I whispered wrapping my arms around myself. "I'm so cold."

"Come inside," he opened the door to the gallery that I'd passed earlier. Inside the lights were low and I could see a small wood stove glowing softly in the distance. "I should reintroduce myself," he said. "We've met before. I'm Theo Manhattan. You'll be safe here until the police arrive."

"I remember you," I said. "Thank you."

And that is how Theo Manhattan saved me the day Marco disappeared into the sea.

CHAPTER 19

"Would you like a hot cup of tea?" Theo said, walking me past the studio displays to a small room in the back with some comfortable chairs and the wood stove I'd seen from the door.

"Yes, tea," I shivered. I felt outside of my body. I'd watched Marco's helicopter fall from the sky but my mind refused to process the information in a way that made sense. This felt like a nightmare, a horrible nightmare. I blinked my eyes twice willing myself to wake. Could I wake? Was it possible that this was just a horrible dream?

I pinched my arm and felt pain. I wasn't waking up. "This isn't a joke is it?" I said, facing Theo. "It's real. This is really happening,"

"I'm sorry, yes," Theo said, his mouth locked in a sad smile. "I know it doesn't seem real. Horrible things seldom do."

He spoke with some authority. I looked into Theo's pale blue eyes and I saw a sadness there that I didn't remember. Granted we'd only met once, the night he and his girlfriend installed the silver tree in the condo, but he looked different to me now. He was a shadow of the joy filled man I'd seen that night.

"Would you like to sit?"

He pointed to an oversized plush chair and ottoman that faced the fire. A half-filled cup of tea sat on the table beside the chair along with an open sketch book with an incomplete picture of a woman laughing.

"Thank you," I whispered, sinking into the soft chair. The sound of the siren grew louder. Red and blue lights flashed dimly into the room.

"You will need to see a doctor," Theo said, placing a china cup on the table beside me. He held a kettle of steaming water in his hand and poured a cup. "You are in shock."

"I'm okay," I said, shivering.

"Here." Theo set the kettle down and placed a soft blanket around my shoulders.

"What is a doctor going to do for me," I whispered, staring at the fire. "I'm not okay, nothing is okay." Sobs shook my body.

Theo nodded and sat on a wooden chair in front of me. "The police will be here soon, the paramedics as well."

"But there is nothing for them to do," I hiccupped. "The bodies are at sea." I inhaled sharply and bit down on my knuckle the image of Marco sinking beneath the waves was too much to bear.

"Paramedics always come when there is an accident," Theo said, swallowing. "No matter what has occurred."

We sat in silence for a moment.

"Why are you being so nice to me?" I asked. "You don't really know me."

He looked at me as if considering his words carefully. "I remembered you from the night I did the installation at Marco's house. Marco was good to me, he was a good man and you were clearly in distress. He would have done the same for me."

"He's dead," I whispered the words sounded foreign to me. "I saw him fall from the sky."

"I know," he said, nodding at me. "You really should allow me to get the paramedics."

The red and blue lights continued to flash.

"They can't help me," I said, my voice thin and high. "The man I love is dead. I know what's wrong with me. He's dead and I want him back." I collapsed in a wave of tears. I pulled my knees in close to my body and wrapped the blanket tight around my shoulders as I cried.

My tea cup sat untouched on the table in front of me.

After a few moments, Theo reached out and placed a hand over mine and squeezed. It was a small gesture but it felt big to me. I nodded at him and mouthed the words thank you.

"Can I sit next to you?" I asked, once I'd recovered enough to speak.

"Of course." Theo scooted over and made room for me on the couch beside him. We sat side by side and not speaking staring into the dancing light of the fire.

* * * *

I awoke with a blanket tucked under my chin. I sat up in a panic the memory of the night rushing over me in a sick wave. Marco. The Explosion. Theo Manhattan. The clock on the wall read 5:00 a.m. I jumped to my feet and almost tripped over Theo's legs. He'd stretched out on the ground by the door sleeping on a pile of blankets to form a make-shift bed.

I stood perfectly still and willed myself to breathe before sinking back onto the couch shaking.

Marco was dead.

The thought hit me like a punch in the stomach. Grief, cold and aching seeped into my bones. I rocked back and forth slowly in my seat, biting my lip to try and keep the tears at bay.

I heard a muffled ringtone and realized my phone had slipped into the cushions of the couch.

I dug it out and answered, my voice cracking. "Hello . . ."

"You're alive," Shea gasped, choking on tears. "Holy crap, you're alive."

"Yes," I whispered. "Marco . . ."

"I know what happened," Shea said. "It's all over the internet. I'm so sorry Odessa. I thought you were onboard too. When I couldn't find you."

I glanced at my call list, I had slept through fifteen missed calls.

"I was supposed to be onboard," I said, the memory of Marco turning me away still stung. But if Marco had allowed me to go with him, I'd be dead in the waters of Puget Sound too. "There was a change of plans . . . Marco told me not to go with him."

"Well, thank God," Shea said. "Where are you now? I'll come get you. I've been calling hospitals, the police, no one has been able to give me anything useful."

"I'm at an art gallery near the marina. It belongs to Theo Manhattan. He took me in last night."

That's when I noticed that Theo had woken. He stood and stretched his hands skyward eyes squinting as he yawned. He gave me a tentative smile.

"Well, I don't know who he is or why that's a good

idea," Shea said. "Why didn't you call me? I'm coming to get you."

"I can drive you home," Theo offered, picking up a set of keys. "I need to head downtown anyway."

"I'll be home soon. Theo will drive me," I told Shea.

"Who is this Theo guy? You are probably in shock still. Please let me come get you."

"It's okay. Theo is a friend," I said. I couldn't explain it but as much as I loved Shea I needed to be with someone who would let me sit in silence. It wasn't totally logical but in a very short time I felt as though Theo and I had shared more than just an awkward evening of conversation. Shea meant well but she would want to talk and ask questions. There would be so many questions that I could not answer.

"I'm okay Shea," I said. "Well, I'm not okay, but I'll be home soon. All right?"

"Okay, text me as soon as you get here."

I hung up and exhaled as Theo placed a fresh cup of tea on the table beside me.

"Thank you, I'm so sorry for inconveniencing you." I glanced around the room noticing a framed picture of the woman with the red hair that had been in the condo. "Please tell your girlfriend, I can't remember her name, I'm so sorry. Tell her that I did not mean to keep you all night. I hope she . . ."

"She won't be worried," he interrupted.

"Well, I don't want to cause any trouble."

"You won't. Grace is dead," Theo said, standing perfectly still. I had a feeling that if he moved he might crack into a million pieces.

"I'm so sorry," I said. Theo shared my grief and pain because he lived it. "I didn't know . . ."

"She died last week," he said, eyes glazed. "A car accident on the Aurora bridge. I was at the wheel."

I said nothing knowing there were no words for his pain. There were no words for my pain either. We shared this bitter knowledge.

"It happened on a Tuesday evening. I've been staying here ever since." He gestured to the tiny room where we had spent the night.

"You live here," I said, noticing how he had already folded up his make-shift bed and placed it in a cupboard. There was a cup with a toothbrush on a table near the bath beside a box of unopened crackers.

"I can't go home," he said. "It's our home. I don't have a home anymore. I'm sorry, you have got a lot on your mind, you don't need to hear about this now." He jingled his keys. "Shall we get going."

"I don't mind," I said, grateful to think about someone besides myself for a moment. "Are you allowed to live here?"

"Bloody hell, no," he said, his accent normally so light and charming had a bitterness to it. "I'll stay as long as I can. I don't know what to do exactly."

"Neither do I," I said, shrugging as my eyes filled with tears.

"I am sorry for your loss and mine," Theo said. "I would undo it if I could, take away all of our pain. But I can say that talking to you has made me feel less alone. I am grateful to you for letting me help you."

"Grateful we are both broken creatures you mean." I gave a half laugh.

"Life has tried to break us," he said. "I don't think you are a broken creature though. Me maybe, but not you. You are strong. I sensed it from the moment I saw you and Marco together. It takes a strong woman to steal the heart of a man like him."

My heart stung at the mention of Marco's name. "I don't feel strong."

"Well you are," he said. "And if you will indulge me one more bit of wisdom."

"Yes?"

"You need to eat," he said, smiling.

"Oh my God, you sound like my friend Shea, always going on about nutrition and low blood sugar," I said, managing a weak smile.

"I'm not going to force eggs and rashers on you."

"Rashers, really? You English and your bloody breakfasts."

"I'll settle for a coffee and a scone," he said. "I'll take you home if you agree to eat and see your doctor today. You need to talk to someone about what you've been through."

"I don't want to talk to anyone," I said, feeling like a child. "Maybe you, I could talk to you."

"Fine then," Theo said. "Coffee and conversation. Let's get you home."

* * * *

I held a coffee in one hand and scones for two in a tidy white bag. Theo drove me home in his car, a restored red mustang. I sat beside him wondering why I trusted him. I barely knew him but I felt safe beside him. Clutching my latte, I sipped the coffee knowing I needed food and sleep. Sleep I craved mostly for the escape. I longed to pop a pill and close my eyes to the pain of Marco's death.

"It's here," I said, directing Theo to park in front of

The Holiday.

"It's charming," he said, looking towards the ivy colored brick. The vacancy sign was out again advertising the apartment next door to mine.

"I don't think I can go home," I whispered. "Marco and I spent one of our last night's in my apartment."

Theo nodded and exhaled. His agreement unspoken I still knew he understood. "Your friend lives here as well?" He asked.

"Yes," I whispered.

"How about we go upstairs, get a few of your things and we find her," his voice was so even so comforting. "I don't think you should be alone."

I nodded in agreement and took his arm when he offered it to me. We walked upstairs. I froze when we reached the hallway on the third floor. My tiny studio apartment was at the far end of the hall, it felt miles away. We walked towards it arm in arm. My chest constricted with every step.

When we reached the open door of the vacant, two bedroom apartment next door I panicked and bolted inside.

"I'm sorry, I can't, I can't go back to my apartment," I blurted. I dropped my hands to my knees and leaned forward lowering my head. I was afraid I might pass out.

"I don't know what I'm going to do."

"You don't need to apologize," Theo said. "You don't need to go back if you don't want to."

"Promise?" I said, smiling up at me.

"I promise." Theo looked up and down the empty hallway of the vacant unit. He smiled what looked like a genuine smile. "This is a nice place," he said, turning to walk down the hall.

"You want to live here?" I asked, my heart pounding as I followed Theo into a large oversized living room with a gorgeous chandelier in the center of the room. The windows were bigger here, the kitchen more spacious and there were two large bedrooms on opposite sides of the room. I was half joking but then suddenly I wasn't. "Seriously, you should live here, we should I mean."

Theo looked at me, his brow wrinkling. "I'm not sure I understand you."

"You have nowhere to live and I can't go home," I said, my voice getting more animated with every statement. "Why not? I can't handle any big changes right now, but I could handle this. I could handle moving here. I need a change but not too much of one."

"You're serious."

"Yes."

"You barely know me," he said.

"I need a friend, Theo," I said, taking both his hands in mind and leading him underneath the sparkling crystal chandelier.

He nodded and looked around the space exhaling. "It seems a bit mad."

"Of course it's mad, but we're both in love with ghosts, where else would you have us go?" I asked, tears filling my eyes.

"If you still feel this way in a week I'll consider it," Theo said, grinning. "You shouldn't make any rash decisions."

"I'm not changing my mind," I said.

"Right, we'll see then," he said, looking around the room. "It is a beautiful space."

"Thank you," I said, still holding his hands in mine. There was a moment when I gazed into his pale blue eyes and wondered if we would be more to each other, but I knew from the start that Theo Manhattan and I were friends and not lovers. We were here to help each other heal nothing more.

"Show me the second bedroom then," Theo said.

One week to the day later, we both moved in.

CHAPTER 20

I got into the habit of working late, very late. Dr. Mike successfully advocated to open our study to more patients. There were countless cases to evaluate and enroll in the new protocol. We continued to succeed. We continued to save lives. When I looked into the eyes of the young patients and saw hope there I felt something close to forgiveness. Marco hadn't wanted to take me away from the life I loved and maybe he was right. I'd never know, he'd still chosen for me which hurt.

My gut feeling about Theo was right. He was the perfect roommate. We saw each other in the morning and chatted across the kitchen table as we shared our morning coffee, but we rarely saw each other at night. We both spent as much time as possible immersed in our work.

Nights were the most difficult for me. I'd wake in my bed and find myself staring at the ceiling remembering Marco's touch, the taste of his kiss, the feeling of his muscles under my fingertips. I'd dream about our nights in his four poster bed.

When it was too much I would knock on Theo's door.

"Rough night?" he'd say, smiling.

"Terrible," I'd say.

The circles under his eyes told the same story.

And then he'd take my hand and we'd sit side by side on the couch watching an old movie on cable TV. We were friends and helped each other carry our grief.

* * * *

About a month after the accident, I came home to see a delivery notice tacked to the door of my old apartment. I froze and stared at the pink slip. It flapped against the door as if waving at me.

No one had moved in yet.

The delivery was probably for me.

I crept down the hall and grabbed the note off the door with my heart pounding.

I was right. It was a notice for delivery.

Someone had tried to send me boxes, not just one but four boxes. I took the notice and called them the next morning to update the apartment number. I also gave them permission to leave the boxes in my absence and notify Billie instead.

* * * *

The next day at work, Billie called my cell.

"Hey, you okay if I let these delivery guys into your apartment?" She asked.

"Yeah, sure," I said, sitting at my desk compiling data in preparation for a meeting with the hospital board. I heard conversation on the other side of the line.

"Actually the delivery guy says they have instructions to assemble the furniture," she shouted over her shoulder. "It's not that bedroom guys, it's the other one."

I looked up from my spreadsheet. "What furniture?"

"I don't know, it looks like a bed you ordered and some sort of artsy tree thing?" Billie said. "Hey, watch the hardwood over there . . ." She shouted. "Where do you want the tree?" she asked me.

My heart hammered in my chest as I pushed back from my desk. "Is it silver?" I asked.

"Yes, I think it goes with those bird cages you got a while back. I thought you gave those away?" Billie said.

"I'm coming home," I said. "Don't let those delivery guys leave."

"You don't need to, I've got this . . . Hey guys Odessa wants you to wait." I heard mumbling. "They have another job I'm not sure if they'll still be here."

"Make them wait," I said, hanging up my phone. I grabbed my jacket and my keys. I almost ran right into Dr. Mike. "It's an emergency, I have to go home . . ."

"I got this," he said, giving my arm a quick squeeze.

"You okay?"

"Yes, I don't know. Thank you," I called, as I headed towards the lobby and the parking garage.

I'd given those bird cages back to Marco months ago, and they'd been hanging on that silver tree which as far as I knew was still in his condo.

When I opened the door to my apartment I could barely breathe.

The apartment was empty and there was the silver tree standing in front of the oversized windows. Sunlight glinted off its branches and the series of bird cages that Marco had gifted me long ago.

My knees almost buckled. Seeing Marco's gifts, I felt as though the thin scab that had formed over my wounds tore open. I opened the door to my bedroom and fell to the ground.

In the center of my room stood Marco's four poster bed.

The four posts almost reached the ceiling. The bed was made with the same gorgeous gray bedding where we had made love countless times.

I stood up and fell onto the mattress the tears coming hard and fast.

Why was Marco's bed here? Did he have a will? My

heart hammering I sat up in his bed wiping my nose. I needed answers. There had to be a delivery invoice somewhere in the apartment or Billie wouldn't have let them inside.

I found the paperwork on the coffee table. It was from a local moving company in the Greenwood neighborhood.

I called their office.

"I'd like some information about a delivery that was just made to my apartment?" I said, giving the woman on the call the invoice number. "Can you tell me who placed the order?"

"Let me see," she said. I could hear typing in the background. "Well this is unusual. The order was placed some time ago, apparently these items have been in storage? I'm sorry were you expecting this delivery earlier?"

"No," I paced back and forth my heart racing. "When was the order placed, what day."

"Let me see . . ." More typing. "Looks like the pieces were packed up on the morning of . . ."

She rattled off a date.

The date Marco died.

"Instructions for delivery came the next day."

"The following day."

"Yes," she said. "Instructions from someone, I don't

know who, there isn't a lot of detail here. I really need to talk to the sales team about taking better notes."

"Thank you, you've been very helpful," I said, feeling dizzy. Looking at the silver tree covered with bird cages I felt as though I had woken from a dream.

There was a white envelope sitting in one of the cages. I opened the cage and pulled out the small envelope addressed to O.

Inside there was a travel itinerary to Mexico, air travel, transportation, and a reservation at a hotel called Casa Flora in the town of Sayulita.

Written at the bottom of the itinerary was a note.

Trust me. Trust us.

Today's date was written on the card.

I couldn't breathe. I sank to the floor remembering Marco's final whispered words to me. I wanted to believe; I was terrified that this was some sort of grief induced fantasy. Dead men don't write letters. Dead men don't book flights to Mexico. I sank to the floor afraid to formulate a thought. Marco had planned this in the days and weeks after he'd died. I was either subject to one of the cruelest hoaxes ever known or Marco was alive.

CHAPTER 20

Casa Flora was a series of small white cabanas with ocean front views and private patios. Cabana #3, the one that the white coated bell boy escorted me too, had a small gazebo outside it's French doors and a private infinity pool protected by walls of climbing ivy.

I stood on the patio, arms crossed in my white sundress listening to the roar of the ocean. I pulled up one of the lounge chairs and sat down on the edge clutching my knees to my chest and tried to calm my racing heart. I hadn't told anyone about this trip. Marco was the only person who knew what he'd whispered in my ear that night.

Trust Me. Trust Us.

I prayed I wasn't making a mistake, that my grief hadn't broken my heart and my mind.

Breathing in the ocean air, I reminded myself that the man I loved had sent me a plane ticket. I needed to trust him, to trust us. I needed to give him a chance to explain. I closed my eyes and concentrated on the love I felt for Marco, willing myself to stay calm and not panic.

"Odessa."

I opened my eyes at the sound of his voice.

Marco Amador walked towards me from the beach. He wore khaki pants rolled up to avoid the ocean spray and a white linen shirt. His skin bronzed and beautiful, he smiled as he walked towards the small gate between the cabana and the ocean.

I jumped to my feet and ran down the patio stairs as he unlocked the gate. My arms were around his neck the moment the gate clicked shut.

“You’re alive,” I sobbed into his neck. “Goddamn you, Goddamn you, you’re alive.” I had never felt so many emotions at once. I was happy, angry, terrified and confused. Most of all I was filled with joy, a blinding, hot joy that poured out of my heart and filled my shaking body.

“I’m sorry, I’m so sorry,” he repeated the same mantra again and again, his voice low against my ear, his lips on my neck, my face, my mouth. Laughing and crying we stumbled backwards up the patio steps our hands all over each other.

“So many questions,” I murmured between kisses.

“We talk later,” he said, his voice husky. “I need you.”

“What happened?”

“Later,” he whispered. I moaned as I felt his hard cock pressing against me. I wanted answers but more than anything else, I wanted this man.

"Take me to bed," I said, my hands fumbling with the button of his pants.

He lifted me in his arms and carried me into the Cabana through the small sitting room and a set of white French doors that led to the bedroom.

I turned to see a four poster bed in the center of the room. Translucent mosquito netting hung from the ceiling draping the bed in a gorgeous curtain.

"Nice bed," I whispered.

"It was by request," he said, placing me on the ground and slipping my sundress off my shoulders. It dropped to the tile floor.

He laid me down on the crisp white linens of the bed. I lay naked before him.

I reached up and unbuttoned his shirt running my fingers over the lines of his tattoo. My body ached with longing for him. I spread my legs and touched myself as he watched me.

"You are the most beautiful woman I have ever seen," he said, his eyes glistening with tears. "I am so sorry for the pain that I've caused you."

"Make love to me and then tell me everything," I whispered, touching myself slowly. I wanted him inside me, I needed to feel his body inside mine, I needed to feel complete.

He nodded and slipped out of his clothes and kissed me softly. His lips against mine he moved down my throat, his hands running over my breasts, teasing my nipples as he worked his way down my body with his tongue.

His tongue played with my navel as his fingers moved between my thighs. He slid a finger inside me as his mouth found my wetness. He probed me with his tongue as he massaged me.

I moaned and arched my back, fingers finding the back of his head I pushed him down harder against my aching pussy. I felt the orgasm building in my core, a tightening energy growing stronger and then he pulled away and I felt his cock between my legs. He held himself above me, arms straight, his hardness suspended between my legs. He was big and throbbing and I moaned as he pressed softly between my legs, teasing my thighs apart he pushed inside my wetness.

"Now?" he asked his voice husky. I opened my eyes and stared into his.

"Now," I reached up and grabbed him from behind pulling him inside me, gasping as he filled me up. I cried out from the pleasure of being with him, and from the pain of losing him. Our bodies rocking together, he pulled my hands above my head, his fingers intertwining with mine as he rocked in and out of me, pressing against me with just the right pressure. My legs spread wide, I wanted to pull him in deeper, to open myself up to every inch of him.

Our breathing in sync we rocked back and forth faster and harder until I couldn't contain the orgasm.

"Now, please now," I screamed as the orgasm rocked through my body with a rippling and aching that made me dizzy. I felt him throbbing and shaking above me and then he collapsed on top of me.

We were dripping with sweat. The heat of the day and our bodies was more than we were used to.

"Thank God for you," he murmured kissing my forehead my lips.

"Never leave me again," I said, grasping his hand.

That's when his eyes opened and he squeezed my hand in return. "We need to talk."

* * * *

We sat on the patio in the early evening light wearing thin cotton robes from the hotel. Marco had made us each a Sapphire Blue drink. He'd had the bar stocked with supplies.

We pulled two lounge chairs to the edge of the infinity pool and sat side by side. On the other side of the pool was the staircase and ocean. We were on a very quiet part of the beach. No one walked here other than the occasional surfer on their way to the more popular waves closer to town.

"Tell me everything," I said, holding Marco's hand with one hand and taking a drink with the other.

"I am sorry I lied to you," he said.

"What happened?" I asked my face flushing with anger. I thought seeing him would take away the feelings of betrayal but they lingered at the surface.

"When I realized that Luis knew who you were, it became clear that the only way to really escape and keep you safe was to make the world believe I was dead. Including you."

"You should have told me."

"I needed you to believe," he said, staring out into the ocean, his eyes fixed on the horizon. "Veronica convinced me it was the only way."

"That's what you were arguing about," I said. "How did you do it? How did you disappear?"

"The pilot and I were not in the helicopter," Marco said, his voice weary. "When Veronica walked you away, I knew you'd be too upset with me to see what was going on. The pilot and I both jumped from the helicopter when it was just off shore."

"You jumped into the water."

"We needed the world to see the helicopter take off, to know I was on board."

"You wanted all those witnesses."

Marco nodded.

"The helicopter was on auto pilot," he continued. "We buzzed the restaurant, took it out to sea where it could do no harm, and then detonated an onboard device that was rigged to make the explosion look like a standard fuel leak. It was all supposed to look like a horrible accident."

"And they never found your body," I whispered. "You knew they would just stop looking."

"In a crash like that there are often no bodies," he said. "It's the ocean, people just disappear."

"I see," I said, looking down at our clasped hands.

"If you had known I was still alive you would not have grieved the way you did."

"I grieved Marco," I said, tears filling my eyes faster than I expected. "I grieved, I sobbed, I wanted to die."

"You helped me convince the world, convince Luis that I was dead. I know I put you though a lot. I knew you wouldn't give up," he whispered. "You had your job, the children to ground you, and now you still do."

"And I don't have you."

“The case against my father is moving forward,” he said. “This will end.”

“So you hide out until that happens? How long are you gone?”

“I am gone until this is done. Marco Amador is dead to the world and until my father is locked up. It is safer for you, safer for me, safer for our future family.”

“Our family,” I said, his words making my stomach flutter. “Marco, how can we be together . . .”

Marco pushed his chaise lounge back and knelt before me. “I need to ask you something,” he said, his voice thick with emotion. “Veronica wanted me to wait even longer to contact you, but I was afraid I was losing you. I was afraid you would move on.”

“You know about Theo,” I said, smiling. “Marco, nothing happened.”

“I don’t blame you for anything,” he said. “You thought I was dead.”

“You know sometimes I wonder why I don’t feel something for Theo. I wonder why I don’t escape in his arms, but I know why. My mind and my body belong to you,” I whispered reaching out to stroke his face.

“I want us to be together, forever Odessa Starr,” he said. He pulled a small box out of his pocket and knelt before me.

"What are you doing?"

He opened the box revealing a gorgeous emerald cut diamond ring. "I'm proposing to the woman I love. Will you marry me someday Odessa Starr? When we are no longer hiding from the world? When we can be together without fear, without hiding?"

I looked at this man that I loved and knew there was only one way to answer. "Make love to me and ask me again," I said wrapping my arms around him. He lay back on the lounge chair and I unhitched his pants hiking up my skirt and pushed my panties aside.

He slid inside me.

"We need a condom," he gasped.

"Get one," I said, moving up and down on his shaft.

I heard him fumbling with his pocket and then he pulled out of me for a moment before lifting my hips again. My body pressed against his I rocked up and down on him riding him with just the right pressure. He buried his face against my breasts and then his fingers interlacing with mine until I felt him slide the ring on my finger.

"Marry me," he said, driving his cock up into my wetness.

"Yes," I gasped shocked at how quickly the orgasm

rocked through my body.

"Say it again," he said, "Again."

"Yes, yes, yes," I came shaking and shivering against the man of my dreams as I promised to be his wife.

* * * *

Sometimes happily ever after doesn't look like you expect it. Marco gave me the diamond ring.

"I can't wear this," I said, before my flight back to Seattle.

"I know," he said, taking a long gold chain and looping it around my neck. He hooked the ring on the chain.

I smiled at the deception.

"I will see you again in a month," he said. "We think this will be over in a year,"

"One year," I whispered breathing in his scent as I pressed my mouth against his throat.

"Can you wait a year for me?"

"I've waited my life for you," I said.

"Veronica will make contact next," he said. "Be nice to her. She means to help," he said.

"I will wait to hear from her and I will tell no one that you are alive," I said. "I know the rules."

"We can do this Odessa," he said, grasping my hands. He dropped his forehead against mine an inhaled slowly.

"I will love you every month as if it is our last, but know I am doing everything I can to secure our future."

"And no one can know you are alive," I said.

"No one."

"Agreed."

And so I made that bargain. I wore his ring around my neck and gave him my heart and my soul. Veronica comes every month and delivers a ticket. So far we've met in Sayulita, Mexico; Lagos, Portugal; and Vancouver, British Columbia. We have yet to be together in the United States, and Marco has Veronica monitoring the apartment. She installed a heavy lock and key system and she often scans the place for bugs.

Theo is still my roommate; now my roommate and friend. I have told him nothing about Marco but he knows that the man I loved is dead. He knows I have fears and need the doors locked at night. I feel bad not telling him the truth but some truths need to be kept silent if they are ever going to be contained.

I want Theo to be happy so I've told him that I'll search for someone for him to love. He loves women, days at a time, he is afraid to get attached but always breaks things off after five nights. It's become almost a joke between us, I call his routine his five night stand.

Somewhere out there is Theo's one and only. I found mine in a world where I didn't believe in love, I found the man of my dreams.

My name is Odessa Starr and I believe in true love. I gave up everything and then lost myself to be with the man I love, and someday I will walk down the aisle, give him my hand, and pledge my life to him. I don't need a piece of paper at this point, he's already mine and I am his. It may not be ordinary, it may not be practical but it's worth it. Someday I'll have the man I love back again and we'll make love in our four poster bed.

ONE YEAR LATER

It was 4:30 a.m. and I had early rounds at the hospital. Darkness filled the apartment and the streets outside were quiet. Theo's door closed, we hadn't seen each other in days. Though it wasn't unusual for us to miss seeing each other, we had separate schedules, and separate lives.

It had been over a year since we'd decided to try life as roommates and I didn't regret it for a minute. Everyone assumed we had started with some hot and heavy relationship and I let them believe it. Sometimes little white lies make things easier. It was impossible to explain to anyone my new found celibacy. Making them believe I'd rebounded in the arms of a hottie like Theo Manhattan made my story much more believable.

I walked slowly down the hardwood hallway, hoping the floor wouldn't creak. A coffee mug balanced in one hand I unlocked the series of locks that Marco had ordered installed in my apartment.

"Morning," I turned to see Theo walking across the living room, his taut belly exposed as he stretched his arms overhead.

"Did I wake you?" I cringed, looking at the clock.

"No, couldn't sleep," he said, rubbing his eyes. He smiled at me that familiar smile full of pain and longing.

"You know you really need more sleep," I said. "I know why I'm up early, what is your excuse."

"Insomnia," he said. "Bad dreams."

"I'm sorry," I said, squeezing his hand. "You need some happiness in your life, you really do."

"I am happy. I have my work and a great roommate," he grinned at me and once again, I wished I could tell Theo about Marco, that he shouldn't give up hope on love. Grace was gone, but somewhere out there was a woman with the depth to draw this man out, a woman who could need him the way he wanted to be desired.

"I ran into Billie yesterday," Theo said, pouring himself a cup of black coffee and starting some toast. He took a travel mug and poured another cup. I knew without asking he was getting me some breakfast, he said I needed to fuel up in the morning if I expected to think coherently at work. "Looks like we may be getting a new neighbor."

"Really, someone new in 304? A guy or a girl?" I asked, remembering my days in the apartment next door. There had been one tenant since I'd moved out, a single guy who was never around.

"A woman," he said, and something about the way

Theo paused made me follow up.

"A pretty woman?" I asked, grinning.

He shrugged and sipped his black coffee as the toast finished. "Beautiful, she was . . ." He paused. "Lovely, quite lovely."

"My, my," I said, reaching across the table to squeeze my friend's hand. "Sounds to me like the great Theo Manhattan has a crush."

"Not a crush, she was just attractive."

"You have not noted a woman's attraction level for a long time my friend."

"I have had lovers. Beautiful lovers."

"Of course you have, and you will have more. I just like seeing that light around you. I like seeing you notice a woman in particular a woman next door. Did you get a name?"

"Callie," he said, shrugging. "Her name was Callie."

I gave him a quick peck on the cheek and grabbed my toast heading for the front door. "I'll be home late tonight," I said. "Don't wait up."

"I never do," he called to me. Theo spent most of his free time at the gallery. He had the gallery, I had the hospital. I had my getaways with Marco and he had his nights with women that always ended in good-bye. In some ways, we were perfectly suited for each other, our lives were set to accommodate each other completely.

Balancing my toast and coffee, I opened the series of locks on the main door.

Billie had accommodated the new locks without issue. She thought my new found focus on security was tied to the post-traumatic stress of watching Marco die. Again, I let people believe what they wanted to believe. Let them see what they want to see. No harm in that.

I opened the door with a start.

Veronica stood outside my door, her cell phone in hand poised to make a call or text.

"What are you doing here?" I whispered, glancing up and down the hall. Veronica's appearances in an out of my life were easy enough to explain. Since she'd been popping up in my work and home life on a regular basis over the past year I usually mumbled vague statements about her artsy background or jet set life and people filled in the blanks.

Again, people see what they want and right now they were seeing something quite odd. It was 5:00 a.m. and I had a visitor.

"I wanted to see you in person," she said, rolling her eyes. "Sorry, I didn't realize how early it was until I got here. I just flew in from Moscow and I'm all upside down. Can I come inside?" she said.

"Theo's here," I said. "He's awake. Let's go to my room."

Theo sat at the kitchen table reading the news on his phone, a steaming cup of coffee in front of him. "Good morning?" he said eyebrows raising as he noted Veronica.

"My friend, Veronica just got into town. You remember her."

"Right, you are the backup singer, on tour or on a break?"

"Exactly," Veronica said, in her lilting South African accent. She linked her arm with mine and leaned her head on my shoulder planting a kiss on my cheek. "I missed my girl too much, I had to come visit." She stroked my cheek suggestively. "Sorry to bother you."

"No bother here," Theo grinned and winked at me. "You two have fun then," he said. "I'll just head back to my room." I felt like a teenage girl being left alone by her bestie so she could make out with her boyfriend without an audience.

"What are you doing?" I said, pulling Veronica into my bedroom. "Theo will think we are lovers."

"Which is exactly what you want since your real lover

is coming to town," Veronica said, grinning at me, her smile wicked. "Tonight."

"Marco is coming here?" I said, reaching out to grasp one of the bedposts. "How is that possible?"

"He is coming to Seattle for business."

"Dead men don't do business," I deadpanned.

"Marco Amador does," she said, shrugging. "Look he is coming to town. I am here to tell you to clear your calendar, the man wants to spend the night with you in this bed." She patted one of the posters for emphasis.

I thought about my nights with Marco and how it had all started in the span of this four poster bed. He had made love to me in ways I hadn't expected, just the memory of our bodies intertwining was enough to make me wet and weak in the knees.

"When will Marco get here?" I asked, instantly all nerves and anxiety. How would I hide him, how would he ever come and go without being noticed?

"Late, late, tonight," she said. "I will make him a copy of your keys with your permission."

"You have a copy of my keys?"

"Of course," she said. "How do you think I got in here this morning."

"So, you knocking on the door was just . . ."

"Me being polite, yes love. I do have manners, don't you forget it."

"Good to know," I sat down on the edge of the bed running my hands across the sleek comforter. We had made love so many times between these sheets. I could hardly wait to feel his skin next to mine, his mouth on my body, my throat, my breasts, and between my legs.

"So, he comes here tonight. Just one night?" I said, my voice thin. "Does this mean we aren't going away this month?"

"No, it means that things are getting better. He should be able to spend a few nights with you. Why don't you have some fun with it, get creative, have a party, excite and explore with your friends, we can sneak him in together."

"A party," I said. "You want me to throw a party."

"Honey, Marco is going to be in your bed tonight, I would think you want to set off fireworks."

I laughed. She was right.

* * * *

Night fell and I lay in my bedroom waiting. Waiting for my phone to beep, for a knock at the door. Finally my bedroom door opened.

Almost midnight and Marco Amador stood in my doorway. He held a key ring in his hand. "I thought it was okay to let myself in," he whispered.

"Yes, yes it is," I said, jumping off the bed. I threw my arms around him closing the door. Our hands could not move quickly enough. He undid the buttons of my night shirt, my fingers on his belt buckle. We undressed as we fell towards the bed, our lips locked together with a fierceness and a tenderness that could not be denied.

I thought about the woman next door for only a moment before we began. His hands on my body I moaned knowing that my voice would shake the walls.

Theo would believe I was sleeping with Veronica.

The girl next door, Callie, that was her name. She might hear me and I didn't care.

"Faster," I said, gasping as Marco licked between my legs, his tongue darting in and out his mouth. "More, more, more."

He spread my legs and slid his enormous cock inside me raising me up, I sat on his lap our bodies fused together, mouths locked, he raised me up and down as I moaned and begged for more.

We came together shaking and quivering. After we lay still I thought I heard a noise next door and I giggled burying my head against Marco's throat.

"Uh oh, looks like we've been caught," I said. "The

new girl next door heard us."

"New girl next door?" Marco said. "Maybe you can set her up with Theo?"

"Are you still worried we may fall in love over breakfast," I laughed, propping myself up on my elbow I kissed Marco's cheeks, his lips, his eyelids.

"No, I know you belong to me," he said. "It never bothers me that your roommate is one of the sexiest men in Seattle."

"I didn't know you'd noticed."

"An inanimate object would notice that Theo Manhattan is hot, Odessa."

"True," I sighed. "You know Theo really does need a woman in his life. He has lovers, he is with women for five nights only and then it ends."

"Only five nights with you," Marco rolled over and propped himself up beside me. He ran his fingers up and down my chest, tracing small circles around my nipples.

"Theo needs more," I said. "Who knows, maybe this woman will be someone special. He noticed her arrival, that's new. He never notices anyone, maybe I'll try to set them up."

"I thought you said he sleeps with women and has lovers."

"They notice Theo, not the other way around," I said. "There is a difference."

"So, you think he just needs true love, the way I needed you."

"Everyone needs to find their true love," I said, smiling and thinking about how much Marco had changed me. If you had told me a year or two before I would be in love with this man, flying around the world for secret rendezvous waiting for the day I could walk down the aisle and pledge my life to him forever, I would have fallen out of my chair laughing.

Marco fiddled with the diamond ring I wore on a chain around my throat. "I want you to wear it tonight," he said, unfastening the chain.

"You do?" I said, swallowing.

"I want to make love to the woman I love while she wears my ring." He took the emerald cut diamond and slipped it gently on my hand leaning over he kissed my fingertips then moved up my body. "Will you still wait for me Odessa?" he said. "I expect it will be soon, but I need to know that you are still mine."

I held the ring up and touched his face the diamond sparkling and casting rainbows on the walls in this room. "I will wait for you forever, I am yours and you are mine."

"Marry me,"

"How many times are you going to ask me that?" I laughed kissing him.

"I'll ask you every time I see you and once we marry I'll ask you every day. Marry me Odessa Starr," he said, his mouth against mine.

"I do," I said, spreading my legs and pulling him deep inside. We made love in his four poster bed again and again that night. We made love and I knew that all the neighbors would hear but I knew it didn't matter. Marco made me complete and someday I would be his wife and we'd spend the rest of our lives loving each other in our four poster bed.

Dear Reader,

I hoped you enjoyed Odessa and Marco's love story.

I have a favor to ask. If you have time, please leave a review for *His Four Poster Bed* wherever you buy books. Reviews are so important to me and other readers. If you do write a review be sure to email me at emmathornebooks@gmail.com so I can send you a personal message to say thank you.

Also, if you want to learn more about the bedroom secrets world and other new series Join my mailing list @ http://eepurl.com/bAf70r for news, free books, and giveaways.

Thank you so much for reading. I hope to share more of the bedroom secrets world with you in the future and other sexy + fun = happily ever after stories.

XO
Emma

Other Books by Emma!
His Five Night Stand – Bedroom Secrets Book 1

Find Emma online!
http://emmathornebooks.com
https://twitter.com/emmathornebooks
https://www.facebook.com/emmathornebooks

Sneak Peek - His Three Piece Suit – Shea's love story

Shea O'Toole believes there are two kinds of men in the world, suits and cowboys. She grew up in Eastern Washington with cowboys and has the broken heart to prove that suits can't be trusted. She made that mistake once.

Troy Van Rossum was just a boy when he lost the girl of his dreams. He's spent the last ten years trying to forget the summer they fell in love but he can't escape the memory of holding Shea in his arms, the taste of her kisses, the heat of their bodies in the night. He'd do anything for a second chance.

When a family crisis strikes, Shea returns home from Seattle to discover that the boy who betrayed her ten years ago has come back and has plans to buy her father's orchards and seemingly destroy her families way of life.

Shea knows that Troy's the enemy, but one look at her first love and all the old feelings come flooding back, the good the bad and the scorching hot.

Shea wants to be strong to protect herself and her family but will she have the strength to resist the man of her dreams and his three piece suit?

Coming in March 2016.

For more sneak peeks and giveaways Join my Mailing list. http://eepurl.com/bAf70r

XO
Emma

About the Author

Emma Thorne's approach to writing romance is that sexy + fun = happily ever after. She lives in Seattle with her smoking hot husband and their two children, a superhero of a little boy, and an adorable baby girl. Emma loves connecting with readers.

Printed in Great Britain
by Amazon